"I'm in this mess because I got shot at, too..."

Keegan cleared his throat. "Where do we go from [unreadable]

"Can you drop me here?" Tracy ask[unreadable] home some other way."

"Nope."

She frowned. "I wasn't asking [unreadable]

"I know, but I'm going to go wit[unreadable] ou. I'm helping. I'm awesome like that."

Again, she shifted. "Keegan, I'm involved in a mess and I'll get out of it. By myself. Do you understand?"

He heard his mama's voice in his head. *Don't be pushy, Keegan. Not everyone gallops through life like you do.* Speed, excitement and danger were the stuff that made life worth living, and too much slow contemplation time could drive a man crazy.

He heaved out a breath. "This isn't something you should face alone. You saw a murder and it's possible the murderer is still out there."

She didn't answer but he knew she was thinking the same as him.

And he knows who you are.

Dana Mentink is a national bestselling author. She has been honored to win two Carol Awards, a HOLT Medallion and an RT Reviewers' Choice Best Book Award. She's authored more than thirty novels to date for Love Inspired Suspense and Harlequin Heartwarming. Dana loves feedback from her readers. Contact her at danamentink.com.

Books by Dana Mentink

Love Inspired Suspense

Gold Country Cowboys

Cowboy Christmas Guardian
Treacherous Trails
Cowboy Bodyguard
Lost Christmas Memories

Pacific Coast Private Eyes

Dangerous Tidings
Seaside Secrets
Abducted
Dangerous Testimony

Military K-9 Unit

Top Secret Target

Rookie K-9 Unit

Seek and Find

Visit the Author Profile page at Harlequin.com for more titles.

LOST CHRISTMAS MEMORIES

DANA MENTINK

H HARLEQUIN LOVE INSPIRED® SUSPENSE

Recycling programs
for this product may
not exist in your area.

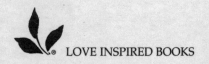
LOVE INSPIRED BOOKS

ISBN-13: 978-1-335-49072-8

Lost Christmas Memories

www.Harlequin.com

Printed in U.S.A.

Bear ye one another's burdens,
and so fulfill the law of Christ.
—*Galatians* 6:2

To Cheryl, a wonderful friend
and an excellent mom to her fur babies.

ONE

Tracy Wilson jerked to a stop in the decorated lobby of the deserted Mother Lode Equestrian Center as a scream died away. At first, she'd doubted her senses. Perhaps it had been the whinny of a horse she'd mistaken for a cry. Then came the thud.

Had someone fallen? A worker unloading boxes after hours? She ran down the hallway to the one open door. Pushing into the dark space, she stopped dead. A figure, tall and wearing black, leaned over a dark-haired woman, hands on her throat, squeezing. Tousled hair screened the woman's face and her hands gripped convulsively, clawing at the fingers throttling her. The attacker was in shadows. Was it a man? Woman? She couldn't tell, but the person looked up at Tracy just as the choked woman went limp, her hands falling away, the life draining out of her. Irises black with hatred locked on Tracy.

The scream of horror died in Tracy's throat as the attacker let go of the victim and dived for her instead. Panic fueled her. She raced back into the hallway, intending to make for the exit, but her pursuer was right behind. In her frantic flight, she knocked over a Christmas tree, sending it to the floor, where it smashed into a mess of silver fragments and gold beads. It did not slow her pursuer.

Tracy knew at that moment she would never make it back to the parking lot. Who could help her? The center was deserted, the Christmas decor gleaming oddly in the dim light. Surely even after hours someone would be around, tending to the horses, the steers? Was there not a single soul to hear her if she screamed for help?

She threw herself at the first door she came to, an office, which was locked. The second door, a storage room, was her only hope. Pulse thundering, she shoved her way inside. There was only a flimsy lock, but she managed to ram a dusty chair under the doorknob.

What she had just witnessed…brutal, incomprehensible, murderous…rocked her to the core.

A fist slammed at the door and booted feet began to kick at the flimsy wood.

Panic bucked like a rodeo bronc inside her. She reached for the phone in her pocket, realizing with a flood of despair that she'd dropped it somewhere. On her way in? In her flight down the hall?

Her clumsiness had always made her father laugh. Now it might just get her killed.

Nerves firing, she searched for a way out. There was no rear exit inside the room, which was cluttered with new supplies for the first ever Yuletide Silver Spurs Horse Show. She yelped as another kick rattled the door. "Help! Somebody help me!" she screamed, hoping the noise would frighten the attacker off.

There was no response except a renewed onslaught of kicks. A chip of wood detached and fell to the scuffed linoleum as the chair shuddered under the knob.

What could she use as a weapon? There was nothing but an old broom, boxes of file folders, rolls of tinsel, cleaning supplies, a folded stepladder. Another vicious kick to the door sent vibrations through the floor.

This can't be happening, she thought. She'd arrived in town only hours before, before making the seventy-mile drive to her newly purchased property in the foothills. She'd never even set eyes on the Mother Lode Equestrian Center until now. After making better time than she'd expected, she'd decided to pop in on the off chance Bryce Larraby, the event's main sponsor, would be there to let her take a peek at the horses she was eyeing for her clients. She'd messaged him that afternoon but he hadn't replied.

Violent memories of what she'd witnessed made her head spin. The killer's fingers throttling, eyes gleaming from the shadows, riveted on her.

A pale glimmer made her look upward. Set high in the wall was a small window that looked out onto the newly erected corrals. It would be a tight squeeze, but she could do it—had to do it.

She dragged the stepladder over and hoisted herself up just as the door lock failed and her flimsy chair barricade with it. She didn't stop to look or scream, legs scrambling up the ladder until a hand reached out and grabbed her ankle. Kicking for all she was worth, she made contact, heard a high-pitched gasp of pain. The effort made Tracy wobble, her cheek hitting the edge of the window frame. Pain seared through her. Flinging the window open, she sucked in a lungful of freezing air and charged through, dropping to the ground, the breath forced out of her.

In a moment she was on her feet again, racing for her Jeep. As she ran she looked for someone, anyone, but there was only the pattering of winter rain and the sound of a horse whinnying. She sprinted, heedless of the crack of thunder and the sizzle of lightning, and finally reached her vehicle. Jamming her key in the lock, she half fell into the front seat. With icy fingers, she shoved her pile of messy blond hair behind her ears and gunned the engine, flooring the Jeep along the road away from the Mother Lode Equestrian Center.

She caught the center's side door fly open in the rearview mirror. Her stomach screwed into a knot as the darkclad killer barreled out. He or she would head to their car, chase her down and murder her before she could report what she'd seen.

You've got a head start, Tracy told herself. *Get on the road, lose yourself, call the police. Just stay alive.*

The faint sound of an engine floated above the storm. The killer was not giving up.

Well, neither am I.

She glanced at the glove box, where she'd locked her father's Smith & Wesson pistol. What prickle of unease had made her decide to take it along on her business trip to the center? Whatever instinct had kicked in, she was grateful beyond measure. All she needed was a moment to unlock her weapon and load it, and she'd be able to even the playing field. It calmed her, if only a fraction.

She took the twists and turns as fast as she dared. The road became narrower, winding past dark hills. Unease ratcheted closer to panic. Where was the freeway entrance? Had she made a wrong turn?

She took the road indicating she was nearing the town of Gold Bar, but it was still some fifteen miles away. There had to be an on-ramp, a main thoroughfare that would get her to the safety of other people. Evening shadows closed in, swallowing up the road in darkness, and she battled back the taste of terror.

The road was hemmed in on both sides by pines. Another time she might have stopped, enjoyed the topography of rippled hills and the distant Sierras still visible in the darkening sky, the scent of wood smoke in her nose. Making friends with some local ranchers always served her well in her career as a bloodstock agent. She evaluated horses and bid on them at auction for her clients, sizing up horseflesh while evaluating the skeletal secrets hidden by the glossy coats.

A cold shiver rippled her spine. Bodies carried all kinds of secrets, she knew, especially human ones.

The sky surrendered to darkness, shrouded by clouds that spit rain on her windshield, but Tracy's pulse thundered with every passing mile. She'd just decided to drive another few minutes in the hope of finding a gas station with a working phone, when the steering wheel shuddered in her grip. Fear choked her. Had the killer caught up? Shot out the tire? But there was no sign of anyone in the rearview mirror, only the irregular flapping that told her she'd run over something and given herself a flat. Not surprising, since she'd been putting off replacing the tires. Why now, though? She slammed a hand against the wheel, poring over her options in her mind.

The rising moon caught the silhouette of a rabbit on the shoulder of the road, wide-eyed, body tense with fear. She knew that fear, too, the sense that she was prey. In a hollow below was an old building, an abandoned train station that had to be some kind of historic relic. With an effort, she sat straighter and squeezed the steering wheel in a death grip.

The killer might catch up with her if she had not managed to shake him off her trail. She desperately did not want to stop, not here in this isolated place, but she could not continue with a shredded tire.

Pull the car into the cover of the shrubs and hide, she told herself. *Wait until you're sure you're not being followed and hike to the main road.* The old train station huddled like some sort of squatting monster waiting for a victim. Every nerve in her body screamed at her to stay away from the festering ruin.

But the heavily overgrown lot offered a hiding place and surely her pursuer would never imagine her stopping in such an out-of-the-way spot. It was either a savvy move or sheer lunacy. Squaring her shoulders, she edged the Jeep off the road, deep into the blackest shadows.

What exactly is a pomander anyway? Keegan Thorn fought against his natural tendencies and kept his motorcycle to the speed limit as he navigated the wet turns that hugged the tree-lined hills. He'd been dispatched by his mother on an errand to Copper Creek and his saddlebag was stuffed full of ribbon he'd secured for the mysterious pomanders, one of many wedding subjects discussed daily in the Thorn family kitchen of late. The Gold Bar Ranch covered one thousand acres, housed some sixty horses and, at the moment, was filled to the rafters with paraphernalia for a Christmastime double wedding.

His brothers, twins Owen and Jack, were marrying the women of their dreams: Ella, a farrier, and Shannon, an emergency room doctor. Although Jack and Shannon were already officially married, this would be the ceremony they'd both longed for, for years. And then there was his eldest brother, Barrett, and his wife, Shelby, who were expecting their first baby in another few weeks, which required additional piles of infant supplies scattered amid the wedding stuff. He grinned. He enjoyed the hubbub and he liked his future sisters-in-law, strong and spirited women both. Shannon, with Jack's help, had recently outsmarted a motorcycle gang bent on murder, so the upcoming wedding festivities were doubly welcome.

Three cowboy brothers married and one with a baby on the way. He chuckled to himself. "Better you guys than me," he said out loud. He approached the turnoff that led to the abandoned train station, grateful that he'd brought his rain gear. He was running late, of course, and his nose was still bleeding a bit after the altercation at the gas station when he'd stopped to refuel.

A shadow from his troubled past had returned. But Keegan wasn't overly bothered by it. He could deal with trouble. He'd been doing that since he was a toddler.

Something flickered in the gathering darkness. He slowed and flipped up the wet visor of his helmet. There it was again—a weak yellow light, like a flashlight beam, bobbing along the gravel path.

Kids probably, teens sniffing out trouble. He knew. He'd done it himself, looked to unleash some of the wild energy that never seemed to dissipate, even after he'd been formally adopted by Tom and Evie Thorn when he was sixteen. He'd spent many hours combing through that abandoned train station, meeting up with people just as wild as himself, doing things he knew full well he shouldn't have done. Drinking, smoking, vandalizing.

Fingers gripping the handlebars, he was about to press on toward home when the flashlight beam was turned upward to reveal a woman's small face, skin luminous in the darkness.

There were two things about the face that kept him there, immobilized. First, her cheekbone was darkened. Though he could not see perfectly, he'd participated in enough brawls to know a shiner when he saw one. Second, her expression, caught in that one spurt of illumination before she vanished into the shadows.

Scared.

Not "I just walked into a spiderweb," but a full-on look of unadulterated terror.

And that was enough to make him pull his motorcycle

off the road and ease it down the gravel path in search of the frightened woman vanishing into the shadows of the abandoned station.

He figured a helmeted guy on a motorcycle would only add to the woman's unease, so he rolled down the slope and parked the bike in the shelter of the empty water tower that glowed eerily in the gloom. After dismounting, he left his helmet on the seat, finger-combed his overgrown black hair away from his face and took the path in the direction he'd seen the woman headed, down to the busted-up platform. He decided she would probably have scooted into the depot, where at least she'd be sheltered from the storm. Where had she come from? He saw no sign of a vehicle, but the station was miles from the nearest building.

He eased through the open door. "Hello?"

Inside, a blast of chilly air hit his face, carrying the sharp scent of rust. The clouds parted to allow just enough moon-light to probe the broken windows, lending weak illumina-tion. The old benches were still intact in some places, as well as the ticketing counter. Branches collected in mold-ering piles and the tapping of tiny claws indicated rats had also found the spot to be a suitable sanctuary.

"Hello?" he said again. No reply except for the rattle of pine needles dropping onto the sagging roof. "I saw you come in."

Still no answer, but his eyes were adjusted now and he saw that the most likely hiding spot was behind the ticketing counter. He had to edge around a place where the floor had fallen out, giving way to a sort of storage cellar some fifteen feet below. One wrong step would lead to a fall that would undoubtedly result in two broken ankles or worse.

This was no place for a lady.

He picked his way carefully around the gaping hole, his

cowboy boots protecting him from the protruding nails and bits of broken wood.

He heard the floor creak as the woman moved behind the counter.

He was about to try the friendly conversation approach for the second time when the woman bolted up over the top of the counter and fired a pistol at him.

TWO

The shot went close, closer than Tracy had intended. She never had been very good with guns in spite of her father's tutelage. The dark-haired guy's eyes flashed shock and disbelief as he stumbled at the noise, falling into a chasm where the floor ought to be. She scrambled around the ticket counter. Her heart pounded, ears ringing from the shot, sick with the notion of what she'd just done. Had she hit him?

This stranger wasn't the killer. His eyes gleamed silvery in the gloom and his shoulders were too broad, but sheer panic had made her fire the gun anyway. She'd meant to scare, to buy time. Had she killed instead? Gripping the pistol, she edged to the crevice in the floor. "Who…who are you?"

She was relieved beyond measure when he answered.

"Keegan Thorn. And that was completely uncalled for when I was just trying to be neighborly."

The man, she saw now as she peered over the broken flooring, was roughly her age, late twenties or early thirties. His black hair was long enough to fall across his brow as he struggled to hold on to the piece of broken flooring that dangled a foot or so down below. He wore a leather jacket and rain pants. His long legs ended in flailing boots. Dark brows framed his eyes, and for a split second she wondered what color they must be in the daylight.

"I...I thought you were someone else. Are you...all right? Um...your nose is bleeding."

"It was bleeding when I got here, from a fist."

Who is this guy? "What are you doing here?"

He looked up at her peevishly. "Well, I thought I was helping you out. I live at the Gold Bar, about fifteen miles from here, and I saw you heading into the train station."

She still gripped the gun, unsure.

"Are you going to shoot at me again or help me out of this hole?"

The question startled her. "Neither. I'm sorry I shot at you, but I have to go. Don't try to follow me."

He grimaced, face contorted with effort. "Why would I do that?"

His questions unsettled her but she steeled herself. "You're a stranger and I'm having a real bad night."

"My night's not going so great, either, and I'm not a stranger. I already told you my name, so help me up 'cause this beam's getting slippery."

The decision twisted her insides. She'd just witnessed a murder. Every nerve screamed for her to run as fast and as far as she could. But she might have killed the guy and maybe he was just what he seemed, a benevolent stranger.

Strangers are dangerous. She'd known that even before she'd seen a woman's life snuffed out. She turned to go, until she heard him grappling for a better hold on the beam.

Something deep down made her blow out a breath, tuck the gun into her pocket, lie flat on her stomach and plunge a hand toward the guy. She managed to help all six-foot-plus of him out of the pit.

He crawled away to a solid section of floor where he

got to his feet. After brushing the dust from his jacket, he fisted his hands on his narrow hips. "Well?"

"Well what?" Tracy said.

"Aren't you going to apologize for almost killing me?"

His smile almost teased one from her until she squelched it. "I didn't. The bullet didn't go anywhere near you."

"Good thing for me you're a terrible shot." He gestured at her coat with his chin. "What else you got in those pockets? A Winchester? Nunchucks?"

"Can I use your phone? Please?"

"Not until you tell me what's going on." He stepped between her and the door, and her pulse ricocheted up a notch. Maybe she'd been right in the first place. She fingered the gun in her pocket.

"Don't come any closer." She was dismayed that her voice came out more like a squeak than a command.

He held up his palms. "Listen, Pockets. I think you owe me more of an explanation, considering. Let's start again. I'm Keegan Thorn. I live at the Gold Bar Ranch. You look like you need help."

Tracy stared. "I have to go."

He folded his arms now, biceps drawing the leather tight. "Uh-uh. Here's what you're supposed to say at this point. 'Hello, my name is—fill in the blank—and I'm sorry for shooting at you when you were trying to help.'" A smile tweaked his full lips.

Model handsome, she couldn't help but notice.

Stop noticing, she ordered herself. *Get help. Get away. Now.* She turned to go around him.

"Who's after you?"

His question stopped her. "I…" Thinking about the hands choking, throttling the victim, made her dizzy.

"You're scared. It doesn't take Sherlock Holmes to see that."

"Look," she said, turning. "I...I'm very sorry I shot at you, but I need to get going, Mr. Thorn."

"Keegan."

"Keegan," she allowed. "I apologize for scaring you."

"I wasn't scared. Just startled."

"Well, anyway, I'm sorry, but I have to go."

"Tell me what's going on, Pockets."

"Stop calling me that," she snapped, nerves twinging. "My name is Tracy."

"Excellent." He wiggled his fingers. "Keep it coming."

Maybe if she could convince him of the urgency, he'd let her use his phone. "All right." She blew out a breath. "Short story is I...I witnessed a murder and I need to call the police. The killer is after me." She hated the wobble that crept into her voice just then.

His eyes opened wide as saucers.

"Now can I use your phone?"

"I'd be happy to let you, but there's no signal here."

She groaned, fighting the urge to scream in frustration.

"But I'll give you a ride to the nearest phone on my bike."

"Your bike?"

"Motorcycle."

She shook her head. "I just need to change the flat on my Jeep."

Puzzlement played across his face. "Why won't you let me help?"

"It's nothing personal." She took a deep breath and let it out slowly. "Mr. Thorn—" She caught his raised eyebrow. "Keegan, I apologize for shooting at you, but I can't explain anything else right now. I need to get away from here. Fast."

"All right. Let's make a deal."

"What deal?"

"I'll change your tire for you…"

"I can do it myself."

"I'm sure you can, but my mama would have my ears for allowing a lady to change her own tire. Anyway, I'll change the tire and ride in your Jeep to the Gold Bar. We can call the police from there and my brothers will bring me back for my bike. It's raining too hard for me to ride safely anyway."

"But…"

"You're soaking wet and scared. You need somewhere to stay for a couple of hours and I want to be sure you get to a safe place. Deal?"

Take the help of a smooth-talking, gorgeous stranger? Trust him, when her life was on the line?

"No, thanks." She ran out the door into the driving rain, strode over to her hidden vehicle and retrieved the lug wrench.

He somehow got in front of her and took the wrench from her hands.

She groaned. "Why won't you leave me alone?"

"Because," he said, the mischievous smile back in place. "You need my help, even if you're too stubborn to admit it."

She stared.

He stared back.

"Is this some kind of cowboy standoff?"

"You got that right, and since I'm the cowboy—" he aimed a long, lazy smile at her "—I figure I win."

Keegan hatched a plan as he pulled the lug nuts from the tire and wrestled the spare into place. Tracy was too scared and untrusting to tell him more regarding her situation, but she would, in time. Keegan would stick by Tracy's side all the way back to the Gold Bar, where his mother would promptly feed her—after her call to the police—and offer her a place to sleep. Before she knew what hit her, Tracy would be spilling the details as if she were one of the family. Evie Thorn's powers of persuasion were legendary.

And then Keegan would fix her problem. Simple. Whoever he was, this criminal would not be terrorizing her again. Keegan would fix it by force if necessary. Part of him relished the thought. Though he'd mostly left his troubled days behind, there was still plenty of untamed energy coursing through his veins. And if there was one thing Keegan could not abide, it was a bully. That sense of intolerance had gotten him beaten up in grade school, but by the time high school rolled around, Keegan had grown to just over six feet of solid muscle and the student body had gotten the message. He would not be pushed around. Period. Nor would anybody he held dear.

Maybe he was born to be a renegade, or maybe it was the adrenaline that came of a birth father who would not acknowledge Keegan or the affair he'd had with Keegan's mother. Or perhaps it was the constant reminders from his half brother, John Larraby, Gold Bar's police chief. Keegan's gut twitched at the thought.

One time late in high school, John had let loose a sucker punch at Keegan's brother Jack and taken him down. Keegan didn't remember the moments that followed, but when his head cleared, he was in the principal's office, nose bleeding, being suspended for roughing up John along with most of the offensive line. No one laid a finger on Jack ever again and that was all that mattered. John hadn't forgotten the drubbing and neither had Keegan.

Tracy's hair gleamed in the dim light, shoved behind her ears and glimmering with highlights that indicated she was a blonde. He liked blondes, but moreover, he liked women who stood right up to him and displayed a strong independent streak. Tracy had already proved herself to be that kind of woman, as she'd hurried to the Jeep and checked the pistol in her pocket.

"Where'd you get the gun?"

"It was my father's. He was…he was teaching me to shoot."

"You didn't finish the lessons?"

"No." He caught the sheen of tears in her eyes, but she swallowed and blinked hard, not about to give him access to her pain. Strong woman, but not strong enough to keep the anguish from peeping through when she'd mentioned her father.

He finished the tire and went to his bike.

"What are you doing?" Tracy called. "Get in. We have to go."

"Gotta get the ribbon," he said as he pulled the package from his saddlebags. "For the pomanders."

She watched him, openmouthed, as he strolled back, package tucked under one arm.

"Pomanders?" she said. "What's that?"

"I have no idea," he said, smiling. "But two of my brothers are getting married at Christmas and Mama says this ribbon stuff is required, so I'm carrying out my duties." He opened the door and tossed the package into her Jeep.

The quirk of a smile twisted her mouth. It was the first time he'd seen her relax even the tiniest amount, and he was happy about it. Anything to keep her mind off whatever nightmare she'd witnessed.

He held out a hand. "How about I drive?"

"Why? You think you're a better driver than me?"

"Undoubtedly, if you drive as well as you shoot."

Another whisper of a smile and maybe the hint of a giggle. Score another one for Keegan Thorn.

"I—" she said just as a rifle blast ripped the air.

Keegan had a split second to grab her wrist and pull her down before more bullets exploded through the night.

THREE

Tracy hardly recognized her own scream. The next shot shattered her rear window.

"Shooter's up behind the water tower," Keegan said. "We've got to—"

He didn't get to finish before the third shot ricocheted off the side mirror and struck Keegan in the shoulder. He cried out, falling facedown onto the wet ground, writhing in pain.

She grabbed his belt and pulled him closer to the shelter of the Jeep. Frantic, she yanked open the passenger door and backed into the seat, hauling with all her strength to pull Keegan in behind her. Somehow he managed to help until they were both sprawled inside. Reaching over him, she slammed the door.

"I guess I'm driving after all," she quipped, earning another groan from Keegan.

"Don't gloat," he said, and she was beyond relieved at his sassy reply.

Slamming the Jeep into Drive, she floored the gas and gunned it up the parking area away from the train station and onto the main road. It would take the killer a few minutes to make it back to his vehicle, and she intended to take full advantage of that time.

She risked a look at Keegan. He was upright, teeth gritted, eyes open, one hand clutching the door handle. "How bad is your wound?"

"No worse than the average gunshot."

She reached for an extra jacket she kept in the car. "Press this to your shoulder."

"Yes, ma'am," he said.

Her pursuer had made it to the road. He was now approaching at a good clip, closing the gap between the two vehicles.

"Keegan?"

"Yeah?"

"Got your seat belt on?"

"Uh-uh. Why?"

"Don't talk. Just strap yourself in."

His eyes found the rearview. "Your killer?"

"Has to be, unless there's an accomplice."

"Name?"

"I don't know."

"You don't know the killer's name?"

"I've never been to this area before," she snapped. "The room was dark and whoever it was didn't exactly make an introduction."

Keegan managed to fasten his seat belt. "The victim?"

"A woman. I couldn't see her face well, either."

She caught his surprise as she pushed the gas pedal hard. The approaching car kept pace.

Tracy's body was tight with fear, foot rammed onto the gas pedal as the Jeep topped seventy miles an hour. Her fear ramped up along with their speed.

She shot a look at Keegan, who was dialing on his cell phone, but she was too focused on driving to pay much attention to the conversation. After a few minutes he disconnected. "Cops are dispatching someone, but I wouldn't hold my breath that they're going to make it a huge priority."

"Why not?"

"First, I'm not sure they believed me, and second, I'm not the chief's favorite guy."

"Why not?"

"He's my half brother, John Larraby. Long story. John's not worth the time it would take to tell you about it."

"Larraby? Is he related to Bryce Larraby?"

"Yeah. Bryce is…" Keegan huffed out a breath. "He's the guy who fathered me, I guess you could say."

She heard rivers of bitterness in his words. "You are kidding me."

"No," he said, craning his neck to check the progress of their pursuer. "You know him?"

Know him? He's the guy I was going to meet. "Tell you later, after I shake him off."

Keegan consulted the side mirror. "Don't be too cocky. He's closing in. You should have let me drive."

She ignored his gibe, shoving down the fear as he repositioned the wadded-up jacket, now thoroughly stained with blood. She had to get help, quickly.

He stabbed a finger toward the darkness on her left. "Slow down. There's a logging road in fifty yards. Turn there, but we can lose him in the foothills."

"I can't drive into the wilderness. That's just what he'd want. He's armed, remember?"

"So are we," Keegan said. "You've got a handgun and I know you're just itching to shoot someone."

"This isn't the time for joking."

"I agree. It's the time for action. Take the logging road. I just texted my brothers our location. They'll find us. Help us."

She floored the accelerator, fighting to keep the wheel

steady as her lungs constricted. "We've got to get to town. Where people are. He won't be able to do anything then."

"Tracy, listen to me," Keegan said. He let go of the jacket and reached his good hand toward her arm, stopping before he touched her. His long fingers were tensed, the nails square and blunt, knuckles threaded with scars as if he'd gotten on the wrong side of a knife a time or two. "I know you're scared, but I've lived here all my life. I know every inch of this valley. We can lose him. Trust me."

His face was carved marble in the moonlight, all angles and strong planes. Trust him? A man she'd known for less than an hour?

There were precisely two men she'd trusted, and her father was dead. Now there was only her grandfather and her determination to carry out the project they'd all three dreamed about. Though she was still anguished that her father was gone not long after she'd gotten him back, she believed 100 percent that God would give her the strength to save herself. And this well-meaning, pushy cowboy was in no way a part of her rescue plan.

"Sorry, Keegan," she said as the car flew past the narrow turnoff. "I have to do this my way."

"Tracy," Keegan said, voice urgent now. "Car's dropping back."

She felt like crowing in triumph. "Good. We're going to make it."

Keegan's tone was ominous. "I don't think so. You'd…"

The blast echoed behind them as their pursuer fired the rifle out the window. The Jeep's rear wheel exploded and the car began to spin.

All Keegan could do was hold on as the Jeep barreled toward the shoulder with a monstrous screech of tires. Tracy fought valiantly for control, but it was useless. The front wobbled and bucked as the tires shredded, turning and spinning until it slammed front fender-first into a drainage ditch. The force of the sudden stop whipped him against the restraining seat belt and then back hard into the seat, igniting fire in his shoulder. With a groan of metal, the rear end of the vehicle tumbled over the front.

In a dizzying whirl, he felt the same sensation he'd experienced when he'd flipped his bike and catapulted himself and his machine over the guardrail as a teen. First the stomach-clenching sensation of dropping, falling. Then the bone-jarring reentry into earth's orbit. *Gravity always wins*, he thought ruefully as his senses came back online.

Something dripped from the ceiling, he believed at first, until he realized he was upside down, suspended by the seat belt, and the dripping was warm and sticky, probably his own blood. His shirt was already sodden from his earlier wound.

He jerked his head toward Tracy.

She was also tethered, but her eyes were closed, hands dangling loose as if she were an astronaut, weightless.

"Tracy," he said, scrambling against his seat belt.

She did not answer, did not stir.

Finally his belt gave way and he dropped to the ceiling, which was now serving as his floor. Tracy's door had been crumpled in the overturn, so he applied his good shoulder to the passenger door. It didn't budge. He switched methods. Three desperate kicks and the thing gave way, dumping him out into the night in a squeal of metal. Still dazed, he struggled to his feet. Judging from the damage to Tracy's side of the car, getting her clear was not going to be easy and he worried about dragging her out the way he'd exited.

The high sides of the ditch in which they'd landed made it impossible to detect anyone bearing down on them. He heard the sound of a car door closing. A smaller vehicle, not a squad car or the heavy ranch trucks his brothers would be driving. Time to move.

Climbing back through the passenger door, he tried to position himself to catch her body when he pushed the button to unfasten her seat belt. She slid into his arms without a sound. Easing her flat, he checked for a pulse with icy fingers. He found one, the steady beat tapping against her smooth throat. He blew out a breath. He should thank God, he knew it, knew his mama would say a prayer, but the urgent desire to take care of things himself dried up the words.

"Tracy," he said, stroking her cheek. He thought her eyelids might have fluttered, so he bent close, comforted by the warm caress of her breath on his face. "Hey, open your eyes for me, Pockets, okay?"

She stirred, moaning as if in pain.

"Gonna have to slide you out of here, but first I'm going to borrow your gun. Don't worry. I'll make sure you get it back in tip-top condition in case you need to shoot at me again." What he would have given just then to see her open her eyes and have her fire a snappy comeback at him.

Just as he removed the gun from her jacket, a series of shots ripped into the back of the vehicle. Sparks flew where the bullets struck the metal fender. He shielded Tracy as best he could, peering around the headrest to return fire through the ruptured window.

He waited for the attacker to come again with another volley of shots. The guy either wasn't much of a shot, or was simply laying down enough fire to keep them in place until he could move in. The next round of shots didn't materialize, but headlights lit up the night, came close and nearly blinded him. Three sets of cowboy boots pounded the ground.

Jack, Barrett, Owen. The Thorn brothers had arrived.

The twins, Jack and Owen, were the first to get on hands and knees and peer inside.

"Gunman," he said.

"Yeah. We saw somebody—" Owen handed his rifle to Jack "—heading for their car." He eyed Tracy. "How bad?"

"Not sure. Ambulance?"

"On the way," Jack said.

Barrett hustled over and assisted Jack in sliding Tracy loose from the car. He draped a blanket over Tracy while Jack and Owen returned to help Keegan climb free of the wreck. His head swam and his shoulder pulsed with pain.

"You hurt?" Owen asked.

"Yeah, he is," Jack said. "Shirt's all bloody."

Owen didn't wait for further details. He hauled Keegan away a few yards, forced him into a sitting position and began searching him for the source of the bleeding.

"I'm all right," he said, trying to push his brother off. Owen, in full-blown Marine Captain mode, ignored him and ripped open a pack of bandages from the first-aid kit he always carried in the truck, then pressed a wad to Keegan's wound.

Biting back a grunt of pain, Keegan squirmed to get closer to where Tracy lay on the blanket. Owen pinned him at the knees with his body weight. "Stop. She's breathing. Pulse, Bear?"

His bearded oldest brother nodded. "Strong."

"Head injury?" Keegan asked.

Owen didn't answer.

"Why are you getting shot at this time?" Jack said.

"I wasn't. She was. Witnessed a murder."

All three brothers stared at him. He wondered what Tracy would think when she woke to a bunch of Thorn cowboys hovering over her.

His heart gave a painful thump at the next thought.

If she woke up.

Owen finally taped a bandage down and released Keegan to go to Tracy's side. He heard the wail of a siren approaching.

"I'll go meet them," Jack said.

Keegan nodded. He recognized the car as belonging to Chief John Larraby, Keegan's half brother and the man he despised second most out of everyone in his life. Better Jack or any of his brothers than him interacting with John.

Tracy coughed and he leaned close. "Hey there," he said softly. "That's it. Open your eyes now for me, okay?"

Slowly, so slowly, her eyes flicked open. She struggled to sit up, but he held her down with a hand on her shoulder while Barrett did the same. "What…what happened?" she whispered.

"It's okay. We got away from the killer."

She blinked, frowning, the dazed look in her eyes awakening a twinge of concern deep in his gut.

"What killer?" she said.

FOUR

She woke from the nightmare, the strong hands squeezing, throttling, killing. Heart slamming, she fought her way to consciousness, waking up with one thought in her mind… murder. Her vision cleared and she jerked to a sitting position to find herself in a hospital bed, startling the three people gathered there. For one long, terrifying moment, she searched her mind and found it blank. Where? How? Who were they? And who was she? Why was an image of murder circling her brain?

"It's okay," the gorgeous blue-eyed man said. His arm was in a sling, a cowboy hat tucked in the crook of the other elbow. A fringe of dark hair framed his face. "You're all right, I promise."

The dull roar in her head quieted just a fraction. The doctor edged forward and smiled. "You've had a little bump on the head. Can you tell me your name?"

Again terror ballooned until facts began to land clumsily into place like heavy stones dropped into a creek. "Tracy. My name is Tracy Wilson."

"Excellent. That matches your driver's license, so we're doing great so far." He asked another round of questions. Slowly she recalled the year, her age, her career as a blood-stock agent. She would have told him of her father if the ache in her heart hadn't stopped her. All the while, she eyed the familiar cowboy and the police officer standing next to him. Police, hospital—it all added up to something bad but she could not command her thoughts.

"It's Friday morning." The doctor's words finally penetrated.

"Friday?" she squeaked. Where had Wednesday and Thursday gone?

"Do you remember visiting the Mother Lode Equestrian Center on Wednesday night?" the cop asked.

Did she? Her fingers curled around the edge of the blanket and she blinked hard.

The cowboy shot a hostile look at the cop. "Can't you let the doctor finish?" There was something difficult between them, something that had started a long time ago, she guessed. The cowboy was beyond handsome, long and lean, a five o'clock shadow darkening his chin. It took her a moment to realize she knew him.

"I've met you, haven't I?"

His face lit with a breathtaking smile. "Yes, ma'am. Keegan Thorn."

Fear bubbled in her stomach as she tried to recall where. The unruly fringe of hair, the deep baritone of his voice were all familiar. Her fuzziness subsided a fraction. He'd helped her, this cowboy.

"I changed your flat tire, but I practically had to arm wrestle you to do it." He grinned, but she thought the smile didn't quite reach through the worry nestled in his eyes.

"Thank you," she said. "For doing that."

He shrugged. "No problem. Happy to help."

"But how did I get a head injury? Was I in an accident?"

Keegan's smile vanished and he looked away. More alarm bells clanged in her mind.

The crew-cut officer inched forward. His blue eyes were

similar to Keegan's, though edging more toward slate than sapphire, but he was a few inches shorter, his face narrow and mouth not as full. There was certainly a resemblance, though, along with the unmistakable tension. A snippet of conversation flitted through her consciousness.

I'm not the chief's favorite guy... He's my half brother.

The cop was staring at her. "I'm John Larraby, chief of the Gold Bar Police Department, Miss Wilson, and yes, you were in a vehicle accident."

The doctor checked her pulse and the bandage on her head. "You were in a crash and you sustained a moderate head injury in the wreck. Things may be a bit jumbled. Oftentimes the most recent memories are difficult to recover at first."

"So do you remember visiting the Mother Lode Equestrian Center in Copper Creek?" John asked again.

She rubbed at the ache building between her eyes. "I remember arriving in town. I think I stopped there." She caught Keegan's eyes. "When did the wreck happen?"

Something in Keegan's expression sent nerves jumping along her spine. "Was someone hurt?" Her body went tense, the action sending the blanket askew. "Did I hit anybody?"

"No," Keegan said, pulling the blanket back into place. "You didn't hurt anyone. I met you at an abandoned train station where you stopped because of your flat tire. We were... I mean...do you remember why we were in such a hurry to leave the train station?"

Again, the flickering images of violence erupted in her mind. Was it bits of a leftover nightmare? "I'm not sure."

The officer tucked his thumbs into his gun belt. "You told Keegan here that you'd been at the center to meet Bryce Larraby." He paused. "You also told him you'd witnessed a murder, but you did not identify the killer or the victim."

Tracy would have leaped from the bed if the doctor hadn't restrained her. The nightmare wasn't a dream. "I did. I thought it was a dream when I first woke up, but it must have really happened. I can remember seeing a man strangling a woman. It must have happened there at the center."

"What man?" John said. "What woman?"

"I…I don't know." She fought against another rising tide of panic. "Did you go there to investigate? To the Mother Lode, I mean? Was there…?" She swallowed.

"We did and found nothing. You never met my father, Bryce Larraby. He said you'd emailed him to set up a meeting, but you two hadn't confirmed a time. My officers finished combing the place. There's no sign of foul play, nothing out of the ordinary."

Tracy stared, mind whirling. Why couldn't she remember where she'd been? Whom she'd seen? Her mind was a mess, but her gut kept screaming that what she did remember was real. It was clear from the chief's tone that he didn't believe her. Her chin went up. She'd learned long ago not to care what people thought of her. "Quietly plow ahead" was her motto. Alone preferably. With others when absolutely necessary.

"Chief Larraby, I'm not a liar. If I said I saw a murder then I did."

"I'm sure that's what you thought you saw. People can make themselves believe almost anything." He paused. "We found medication in your bag. Topiramate."

She sucked in a breath.

"Wait a minute," Keegan said, mouth tight. "What are you implying? She's just been through a head injury, John."

"I'm well aware."

Tracy let out a long, slow breath. "Those pills are for seizures, Chief Larraby, and I haven't taken any lately."

"How do you define *lately*?"

"I haven't had a seizure in more than six months, which is why I can drive." Her tone was cold and she hoped he got the full impact of her distaste for his questions. "I've been tapered off the meds under a doctor's care. I carry them because my property is in a remote area and I haven't found a local doctor yet. I'm not an addict, and whatever I witnessed wasn't a product of drugs. That much I can tell you for certain."

"Confusion, short-term memory loss." John ticked the items off on his fingers. "All symptoms of overuse. And the medication, Topiramate—it's used to treat alcohol addiction, isn't it?"

"Knock it off." Keegan's tone was savage. "We got shot at both at the train station and the road just before we crashed. That's fact, and you can't gloss over it."

Tracy gasped. Shot at?

"We've examined the scenes and the car," John said coldly, "but we've got nothing on the shooter except some tire tracks. Doc, can you run a blood test to check for drugs in her system?"

"That's—" Keegan started angrily.

"That's perfectly fine," Tracy said, cutting him off. "Go ahead."

"I can run them, of course," said the doctor. "But most will only stay in the system for two to three days, so you may not find anything anyway."

"Run the tests," John repeated. "We have to check out her story."

"It's not a story," Keegan snarled. "Stop treating her like a criminal."

"I'm doing my job and you need to back off."

Keegan's eyes flashed blue fire. "No, you're not. You're punishing her because I helped her. Or maybe you're trying to cover up for one of dear old Dad's employees. Is that it? Does Bryce have some skeletons over at the center he's pressuring you to bury?"

John whirled to face him, hands fisted. "Keegan…"

"Gentlemen," the doctor said. "She needs rest. Your visit is over."

"I have more questions," John said.

"They'll wait. Out." He ushered them to the door.

John followed the doctor into the hallway and Tracy could hear him begin a conversation on his cell phone.

Keegan stopped and turned before he cleared the door.

"I'll be waiting out in the hall in case you need anything." He lowered his voice. "I think they've refilled the free cookies at the nurses' station by now since I ate the last six. Not homemade, but they'll do. I'll sneak some in for you." He turned to go.

"But…" She didn't know where to begin. Her memory was as ragged as an old coat—they'd apparently been shot at. "Someone tried to kill me? And you got shot because of it? I don't understand all this. Why can't I remember the murderer's face? The victim's? What is happening to me?" To her dismay, tears flooded down her cheeks and she bit her lip to keep from outright sobbing.

He was at her side in a moment, tender and soft. "Hey there, Pockets. Don't worry. Soon as you get some rest, we'll figure it out, okay?"

Pockets? His hands were strong as he brushed at the trickle of tears.

"We're…friends?" she found herself whispering. Friends were not something she sought out. Too much disappointment down that road after she'd seen her closest friends abandon her when the truth came out about her father. His shame had cloaked her like a stain, it seemed, friendships abruptly evaporating when he'd been sent to jail.

Focus on Grandpa. Get out of here.

Still, there was something so warm in Keegan's touch. She allowed herself to feel comfort in it, the solace of knowing he wanted to protect her. It was a new feeling, both delicious and unsettling.

He grinned widely. "Yes, ma'am, we're friends. I mean, you tried to shoot me and all, but once we got that out of the way, we bonded like two horses in a snowstorm."

"I...shot at you?" She gazed in horror at his arm. "Did I do that?"

"No, ma'am. No offense, but you're not that good a shot."

"I'm not?" she said weakly.

"Nope. You probably couldn't hit the broadside of a barn, as my brother Owen would say."

Her small giggle surprised her. "That's exactly what my grandpa Stew would say, too. He's an old cowboy from way back. When he had to sell his land, it nearly killed him." She chewed her lip. "He's arriving tomorrow, Saturday. I have to get out of here to meet him." She looked around. "My cell phone. Have you seen it? I have to call him. I think I lost it somewhere."

He leaned down and caught her eyes with his. "You didn't have one at the train station, but I'll ask the doctor anyway. Don't worry. I know you're scared, but it's gonna be all right." He winked at her. "I promise, and I always keep my promises."

How could she believe that? She didn't even know the man, not really, but she found herself clinging to the idea that Keegan Thorn might be what he said he was: her friend. It wouldn't hurt to have a friend right about now when she seemed to have garnered an enemy in John Larraby.

The doctor stuck his head in, voice stern. "Mr. Thorn, when I said it was time to leave, I meant it."

"Sure thing, Doc," Keegan said, giving a lock of her hair a playful tug. "I'll be right outside, Pockets."

"Why did you call me that?"

He grinned. "Oh, that's a story for another day. And trust me, you're gonna love it."

Despite his playful words, fatigue and worry pressed down on her as the door closed softly behind him.

Tracy was released late that afternoon and Keegan was ready. She could not drive for three days due to her head injury, so Keegan took one of the ranch trucks, having discarded the sling as soon as he was out the hospital doors.

"I really think you should come and stay at the Gold Bar," he said as he opened the passenger door for her. "There's room. My brother Barrett and his wife, Shelby, are living in her uncle's house and tending his ranch while he's in Europe since their own place isn't done yet. Something about grout and shutters."

She climbed in gingerly, wincing, and he realized for the first time how petite she was, the top of her head coming only to his collarbone. "I can't remember much more, but I did recall something to do with celebratory pomanders."

He chuckled. "Double wedding. Pomanders are for that. Baby coming, too, for Barrett and Shelby."

"That's enough without squeezing in an addled stranger."

He climbed into the driver's seat. "You're not addled. The doctor says you're likely going to get your memory back in time."

She bit her lip, a look of fear flickering through her hazel eyes. Her blond hair was tucked behind her ears, revealing scratches and a bruise along her jawline. Her profile was so delicate, he marveled at it.

Aww, knock it off, Keegan. She just needs someone to keep her safe and get John off her back until she regains her memory—a friend, nothing more.

Keegan had never been short of friends, especially female ones who loved his reckless pursuit of fun and his "barn burner" attitude, as his adopted mother would put it. And that was all he required of his relationships: companionship, shared interests and a zest for adventure. He was too restless to look for anything deeper.

He realized she was looking at him.

"Oh, sorry, did you say something?" he asked.

"No. I'm the quiet type, but I…I mean…" Her fingers twisted together on her lap. "I'm very sorry for shooting at you. I can't imagine why I did that."

"Plenty of people would line up to take a shot," he joked.

Her eyes went wide. "Really?"

"Well, maybe a punch rather than a shot, but you get the drift. I got one particular gang member who would love to lay me flat. Sonny B, he goes by."

She nodded, more out of politeness than understanding, it seemed. He'd probably scared her.

"I lived a wild youth. I'd like to say I'm reformed, but the jury's out still." Exiting the parking lot, he headed for the main road. He'd figured she'd be too well mannered to ask, and he was right.

The winter sun was low in the sky, glaring through the windshield as they drove west, so she pulled down the visor. Three plastic-wrapped sticks of beef jerky fell into her lap.

"Good catch." He laughed. "Snacks. I'm always hungry. Want one?"

She laughed. "Maybe later. I'd really appreciate a ride to my property, if it's not too much trouble. It's up in the foothills."

He shrugged. "Suit yourself. Give me directions."

"About seventy miles east. I just bought it two months ago."

Though he asked a few questions, she kept her answers vague. Didn't trust him, and maybe she was right not to. Strange guy, strange town, bullets flying and a murder she couldn't remember.

She toyed with the zipper on her jacket. "Keegan, you've been good to me. I don't want you to think… I mean…what John said about the pills… I was thrown from a horse and I had a series of seizures for a period of time. I didn't…"

He put his hand on her forearm, surprised at the delicacy of the bones there. He could circle her entire wrist with two fingers, yet she'd fired a gun at him, so the size of her spirit outstripped everything else. "I know you aren't abusing."

She looked at him full on. "But how can you know that when you don't know me, not really?"

Secrets flickered deep down in her eyes and he suddenly realized that her past might just be nearly as complicated as his own. Complications were things he usually avoided, but he felt an urge to dive right in to her messy situation and help.

She didn't ask, Keegan. Cool your jets.

"Maybe I don't know you well, but John is a jerk and he'd happily discredit you in order to preserve dear old Dad from embarrassment."

"He's a cop, surely…"

"He's a jerk, trust me." The words snapped out harsher than he'd meant, so he gave it a beat before he continued. "You were beyond scared when I met you at the train station—terrified because you'd witnessed a murder. And that wasn't due to alcohol or pills."

She shot him a nervous glance. "Do you really believe that?"

"Yes, I do."

Again the shadows flittered across the hazel irises and she looked away, wrapping her arms around herself as if she was cold. He flipped on the heater.

"But how could there be no sign of it at the center?"

"Because someone is trying to cover it up, and I'm going to find out who that is."

Tracy straightened. "I appreciate it, I really do, but you've done enough. This isn't your fight."

"Yes, it is."

Her jaw went tight. "Please don't dive into my problems because it's a way to even the score with your brother."

Her tone was soft but the words cut right to his core. Was that what he was doing? Why he'd stayed in the hospital after his wounds had been treated?

No, this wasn't about revenge; it was justice he was after. Justice for both of them.

It was an effort to keep his voice calm. "I'm in this mess because I got shot at, too." *But if my father is covering up with the help of my brother, he's not going to get away with it.*

He cleared his throat. "Where do we go from here?"

Her gaze drifted to the turnoff that led to the Mother Lode Equestrian Center. A frown creased her forehead. "Can you drop me here instead? I'll get a ride from here some other way."

"Nope."

Her frown deepened. "I wasn't asking your permission."

"I know, but I'm going to go with you. I'm helping. I'm awesome like that." He made the turn, the truck rolling by acres of grass just starting to turn green after the first of the winter storms.

Again she shifted. "Keegan, I'm involved in a mess and I'll get out of it. By myself. Do you understand?"

He heard his mama's voice in his head. *Don't be pushy, Keegan. Not everyone gallops through life like you do.* Why they didn't, he couldn't imagine. Speed, excitement, danger was the stuff that made life worth living, and too much slow contemplation could drive a man crazy.

He heaved out a breath. "This isn't something you should face alone. You saw a murder and it's possible the murderer is still there."

She didn't answer but he knew she was thinking the same as him.

And he knows who you are.

FIVE

Tracy hopped out of the truck before Keegan could come around to open the door for her. Her brain screamed that she was crazy to go back into the Mother Lode Equestrian Center. Her father's favorite saying rang in her ears. *There's no way around the trouble but through it.*

Chin up, she pushed through the door into the lobby, both anticipating and dreading what her memory would dredge up. She wiped sweaty palms on her jeans as two men walked up to greet her. An older man with salt-and-pepper hair, his handsomeness undimmed by his sixty-some years, looked up from his conversation. He wore khakis and a long-sleeved sweater, which evidently meant he wasn't too hands-on with the horses. He glanced from her to Keegan and his smile flickered for a moment.

Keegan said, "This is Tracy Wilson."

The older man's eyes widened and his mouth opened in surprise. She caught it then, the resemblance between the two in the unguarded expression. Father and son? "I... well, I'm not sure what to say other than I'm glad you are all right, Miss Wilson."

Tracy's pulse pounded as she searched her brain for any flash of recognition. "Thank you," she said faintly. "We exchanged emails. I was... I...I intended to come and see

Flight of Fancy, the horse my client is interested in." How could she possibly remember that fact and forget so many other details? She hoped the exasperation didn't show.

The other man with Bryce Larraby stepped closer. He had dark, neatly trimmed hair and a close-cut beard, and wore jeans and a long-sleeved work shirt in a soft material. "Mitch Arnold," he said, extending his hand. He gripped her fingers, one palm covering their joined hands. "Pleased to meet you."

Bryce recovered. "He's the bull breeder, supplying the animals for our rodeo event."

"Best bucking bulls in the country," Mitch said with a grin.

After another moment he released his grip as a young woman entered from the back room. A mop of curly brown hair framed her full cheeks, gold drop-pearl earrings glinting in the nest of curls. She stopped short when she saw Tracy. "Oh…hi."

"This is Regina Parker," Mitch said. "My fiancée. She works in the stables. Regina, this is Tracy Wilson. She's evaluating Flight of Fancy."

Regina raised an eyebrow. "Oh, the bloodstock agent."

"Yes." Tracy detected something disapproving in Regina's tone. "I'm sorry. Have we met?"

"No. It's just…well, my brother got ripped off by a bloodstock agent before. Got him a horse with ligament damage and earned a fat fee from it. Disappeared after, of course."

Tracy kept her smile even. "I'm not that kind of agent. You can check my references if you like. I'm here to see Flight of Fancy."

Bryce took a step forward. "Of course she's a quality bloodstock agent, Regina. I love Flight of Fancy. He's got such personality." Bryce nodded at Regina. "Bring him to the arena for Miss Wilson now, okay?"

"Yes, sir," Regina said and exited the same way she'd entered.

"This is awkward." Bryce offered an apologetic smile. "I would rather not bring it up but…" He stuck his hands in his pockets. "The police have been here since Wednesday night and, well, I'm afraid there's just no sign of any violence."

Tracy's face went hot as she caught the look from both men, a look that said she was some sort of nutcase. "I know I saw a murder." *Even if I can't remember the killer's face.*

"And someone shot at both of us," Keegan added. "Kinda lends credibility to her report."

Mitch quirked an eyebrow. "Problem is, we got no body. So who was murdered, exactly?"

With all eyes locked on her, Tracy wished she could sink into the floor. It brought back her miserable high school year when her father had been released from jail, where he'd served time for assaulting his former business partner. The whispers, the looks, the comments like "her dad's a criminal," all came rushing back in a wave of shame that made her legs go wobbly.

But she'd forgiven her father, even if her mother couldn't, and he'd accepted his forgiveness from the Lord. That was the past.

She steeled her spine. "I saw a woman murdered. I can't remember her face or the killer's, but I will, and when I do, someone is going to jail."

Bryce jerked as his phone buzzed. "That's Regina. The horse is ready for you to look at." He glanced at Keegan. "I know you'd be pleased as punch if something shady happened here, anything that would tarnish my reputation and the Mother Lode's, but nothing did. A lot of folks are counting on this horse show for their livelihoods, for the excitement of it and what it brings to our town."

Keegan shook his head. "Spoken like a true politician with plenty of skin in this game, Mr. Mayor."

Bryce frowned. "And you, Keegan? Entered into the cutting competition, I noticed."

"That a problem?"

"No."

Mitch chuckled. "Family drama. Better than television."

Keegan stared at him and Mitch held his gaze.

"Just joking, man," Mitch said. "Don't take it personally. I got a chip on my shoulder about my old man, too. Comes a point you gotta let it go."

"This doesn't concern you."

"I'm only concerned about what impacts my paycheck. Just don't go looking for trouble where there isn't any, and we'll all get along fine."

Bryce and Mitch left together.

Trouble where there wasn't any? Tracy took in the angry pinch to Keegan's mouth as he stared after his father and Mitch.

Oh, there's plenty of trouble here already, she thought—trouble she wanted nothing to do with.

Tracy strode away a few paces to gather her emotions, Keegan figured. He needed a moment to collect his, as well. Even just being near his father brought it all back: his abandonment of Keegan's mother, his flat-out accusations that she was a liar until the paternity test proved him to be the father. Keegan had been ten at the time she'd forced the test, the beginning of his mother's battle against breast cancer. She'd gotten a pittance of child support out of Bryce Larraby by the time she'd lost her life to cancer when Keegan was sixteen. Father Dearest hadn't even had the decency to attend Keegan's mother's funeral.

He forced his fisted hands to relax and went after Tracy.

Standing next to a decorated Christmas tree, she looked even smaller. As he came up next to her, she gasped, arms rigid as if she'd received an electric shock. He wondered for a moment if she was about to have a seizure, so he reached out for her, but she grabbed him first, hands clutching his forearms, face stark white.

"I remember this tree. Keegan, I remember it."

He could feel the cold from her fingers seeping through his shirtsleeve. "What exactly? Tell me."

"I remember running by it. I was scared. Terrified." Her mouth was tight with the memory. "He was after me—the killer. I brushed by this tree and an ornament fell off and broke. It was a silver ball with gold beads glued onto it. It shattered on the floor."

"Can you remember his face? The guy who was after you?"

She closed her eyes, breathing hard. After several seconds she opened them, deflated. "No," she said. "I can't."

He let her breathe a few times to expel some of the fear before he gently pushed her aside and started hunting around the bottom of the tree. "Maybe there are shards. It won't be proof enough for the cops, but let me see if I can find a piece to corroborate your details."

Underneath the tree was a flannel tree skirt in a bright holiday plaid, which concealed a water reservoir. Other than a pile of needles and an ornament hook, he found nothing, no sign that anything had broken.

She studied the branches. The ornaments were laid out at precise intervals, all silver orbs with gold beading, except for one. It was a subtle difference, but the one nearest the bottom was a plain silver ball.

"Someone replaced it," Tracy said.

Keegan grabbed a tissue from the box on the reception counter and reached for the ornament. "I'll put it in a bag and have it checked for prints. I have a friend who can do it."

"No, you won't."

They whirled to find John Larraby glowering down at them. "That's my job. I'll do it, if you give me a reasonable explanation of why I should bother."

"I broke it as I ran, and someone hung a new one in its place," Tracy told the chief.

"You remember that detail now?"

She nodded.

Regina called to them from the doorway. "Are you coming, Miss Wilson? The horse is ready."

Keegan put an arm around Tracy's trembling shoulders. "You don't have to do this."

She swallowed hard. "I'm okay." Gently she detached herself from his grasp. "I'm ready," she called to Regina, following her out the front doors.

John grabbed another tissue and retrieved the ornament from the tree.

"Be sure it doesn't get lost," Keegan said.

John's expression hardened to cement. "Don't mess with me, Keegan."

"I wouldn't dream of it, brother, not unless you give me reason to."

Keegan thumbed back his hat and walked away.

Tracy tried hard not to show that her knees were still wobbly as she followed Regina to the arena. She took a stab at being friendly. "Have you worked here long?"

"Since they broke ground. I tend to my stable duties and Bryce put me in charge of the front office part-time."

Pride crept into her tone. "I love it, love my work. Even met my fiancé here, plan to stay forever, if they'll have me."

"Congratulations on your engagement. Do you have a date picked out?"

"Not yet. Things keep getting in the way." Her tone was dark. "Why do you care anyway?"

"Just being friendly."

The woman rounded on her. "Let's cut through the garbage, shall we? You're an outsider. You have no reason to be friendly to some stable hand you just met. So what are you after, exactly?"

"After?"

"With this murder story. What are you angling for? Money? From Bryce Larraby?"

"I'm not after anybody's money. I'm telling the truth."

Regina hooked her thumbs in her belt loops. She was tall, arms wiry and muscled, dark eyes brimming with anger. "Just so you know, Bryce Larraby is a great man. He's done awesome things for this town and me personally. Busted my wrist in the summer doing some rock climbing, and he kept me on and even paid me while I was on leave. Every single person who works here would do anything to protect him, especially me."

Anything? Including lying about a murder? She stood straighter. "I want nothing from Bryce Larraby."

"Yeah? Coming here with a story that could tarnish our event? With Keegan, who's got a massive chip on his shoulder?"

"Like I said, I told the truth and I have no ulterior motive."

"Well, Keegan does—he'd love to destroy Bryce, so keep that in mind. Mitch told me all about how his mother tried to weasel money out of him after she seduced him while he was married to John's mother. He'll use you and anyone else to get back at his dad."

Use you. She looked at Regina full on. "Thank you for your advice. Now I'd like to get to work, if that's okay with you."

Regina shook her head, which sent her earrings flashing gold against her curls. "I have some chores to do. See your own way out when you're done."

Tracy tried to get her rapid breathing under control. How had she earned herself another enemy already? That had to be some kind of a record.

She knew part of Regina's comments were true. Keegan did have an enormous chip on his shoulder. *He'll use you... to get back at his dad.* If that was true, it was a top-notch reason to get her business done at the Mother Lode and get out.

The arena was clean and well lit, the electric lights on the vaulted ceiling overhead illuminating the soft dirt floor, which was newly raked, from the looks of it. On one side of the arena was a towering stack of baled hay that lent a fresh smell to the space. She breathed in deeply to calm herself. She was in her element here with the horses and hay. She approached the beautiful stallion standing next to the bales, craning his neck over the fence in search of a snack. Flight of Fancy was as gorgeous as the photos she'd seen when she'd researched his bloodline. His conformation at first glance was excellent, as well. Flight had already fathered two offspring that had proved themselves worthy dressage horses.

"Hey there, pretty boy." She gave the horse a moment to get used to her proximity before she reached out to stroke his neck.

Keegan joined her and she was pleased that her fingers did not shake as she caressed the animal. Keegan was close, very close, and her pulse would not behave for some reason. *He's probably using you, remember?* But his smile was so genuine, his presence so comforting. A few stable hands milled about, but the arena was empty except for the two of them and the horse.

"He's a looker," Keegan said.

"Yes, he is. My client is interested in a stallion to breed with her mare. She wants a dressage horse. It's her passion." She caught his snort. "Dressage not your cup of tea?"

"No, ma'am. I'm a cutting-horse man. Horses were meant to help on ranches, not jump over little white fences."

She laughed. "That's very snooty, Mr. Thorn. Dressage dates back to classic Greece when they trained horses to do evasive maneuvers for battle. Don't knock it until you've tried it."

"I'll pass. I'd look pretty silly in those tight white pants and the shiny boots."

She looked down at his well-worn cowboy boots and long legs covered by faded denim and decided he was probably right. Keegan Thorn was a horse of a different color for sure. Turning her attention back to Flight of Fancy, she took his lead rope. "Let's see about your gait, boy. Are you as good as you look on your YouTube videos?"

"Let me," Keegan said. He took the rope from her and led the horse away.

The horse's natural walk was perfect, and so, she noticed, was Keegan's. He had a brisk, easy way next to the horse that was somehow masculine and graceful at the same time. A natural athlete, she supposed. She leaned back on the fence and admired the power in both of them. Something trembled against her back. For a moment, she thought it must be an earthquake.

Keegan's mouth dropped open. "Look out!" he shouted.

Still uncertain what was happening, she glanced up in time to see the tower of half-ton bales begin to topple.

Her scream froze in her throat as the bundles hurtled down toward her.

SIX

Keegan released Flight of Fancy and charged toward the falling bales. A cascade slammed into the ground with brutal force. One split its twines and sent hay in all directions. Tracy had managed to dodge to the side, but she was still in the path of the falling loads.

One lunge and he had her around the waist, yanking her farther out of the way of the tumbling stack. A bale thumped his back as it slammed onto the arena floor, dirt exploding around them and hay bursting from the six-foot-wide bundle. The impact knocked them both to the floor.

He caged himself over her body, protecting her as best he could, his shoulder twinging with the effort. Another bale caught him in the side, nearly tossing him away, but he held firm against the force. There were shouts that he barely heard over his thundering heart and labored breathing. Feet plowed up more dirt, but he could not see clearly around the haphazard piles of hay and the shower of flying dirt. He closed his eyes against the onslaught of debris.

Tracy. How much impact had she taken before he'd dragged her aside? He only knew she was alive because one hand clutched his bicep. She was so petite, and only just out of the hospital. Above them the bales shimmered in his grit-filled vision and he couldn't be certain no more were about to come down. He braced himself. If he took a full-on hit from a half-ton bale of hay, that would be the end of them both, but at least he'd go out giving it his all.

After what seemed like a lifetime, the vibrations stopped as the bales plopped into their final positions. A few still teetered on the edge of the pile. He heard shouts, the scuffling of boots.

"What happened?" His brother John appeared, yanking a fallen hay bale aside to find them. "I was on my way to my vehicle and I heard yelling."

Keegan ignored him, his attention on Tracy.

"Are you hurt?"

She was inches from him, hazel eyes wide. She tried to answer but nothing came out. Was she injured? In shock?

"It's okay, just breathe. In and out. That's good." He stroked a thumb over her cheek. "Take your time." Inside he was not the slightest bit patient, waiting to hear if she was hurt in some way. His gut was cinched tight.

After a couple of unsteady breaths, she shook her head. "I… No. I'm not hurt. At least, I don't think so."

He eased off and helped her to sit up. There were bits of hay in her hair and dirt smudges on her shirt. Bryce Larraby, Mitch and Regina had joined them from somewhere, and stable hands scurried to secure the remaining bales.

Keegan brushed another smudge from her cheek. "Sure?"

This time her nod was more certain. "You?"

"I'm okay."

"Your shoulder…"

"Tough as shoe leather," he said, giving her a wink.

She smiled then jerked. "Flight of Fancy? Was he…?"

"Aww, that stallion left me in his dust getting out of the way. He's fine, laughing at us, I think."

In truth, a stable hand was holding on to Flight's lead

rope, calming the animal whose ears were pricked with tension.

Keegan got to his feet and shook the hay from his arms. He helped Tracy up, an arm around her waist in case she'd incurred an injury she wasn't aware of.

"I said, what happened?" John demanded again.

Bryce wiped a hand over his forehead. "I can't believe it."

Keegan rounded on them both. "Pretty clear what happened. Can't you see?"

"What are you implying?" His father's brows were knit into an angry line.

"I'm not implying. I'm saying it straight-out," Keegan said. "Someone pushed over the bales."

"No," Bryce said. "I'm sure it was an accident. They were improperly stacked."

"No, they weren't," Regina said. Keegan noticed a flush spread across her cheeks. "I supervised the stacking myself. Bales with broken twine were used as feed, not stacked. We kept to the safe dimensions and loaded them plumb and square. I did my job."

"We weren't accusing you," Tracy said.

Regina folded her arms. "That's what it sounded like."

Mitch tapped her arm. "No slight to you, girl."

Keegan smirked internally at that one. Both his biological mother and his adopted one had taught him a woman was never to be called a girl. Ever.

Regina did not look at him, arms folded tight across her chest. "It wasn't my fault."

"No, of course not," Bryce said. "It was just a freak accident. Likely the stack was unsettled by something, or a couple of bales in the middle failed."

"That's not what happens with hay," Keegan said.

"Oh, that's right," John snapped. "I forgot we were in the presence of Cowboy Keegan here, hero of the West."

Keegan stared him down. "I'm not ashamed of who I am or where I came from." He paused. "Are you?"

John flinched, and Keegan knew his arrow had struck home. His triumph outweighed the sliver of guilt. Dear old Dad hadn't stayed with John's mother, either, the woman he'd been married to while cheating with Keegan's mother. Keegan's mom hadn't even known Bryce was married. At least Bryce had taken care of John's mother in the divorce. Better than he'd treated Keegan's mom, who'd only gotten child support because the courts had forced the issue. John had taken every opportunity to bad-mouth Keegan's mother and tell anyone who would listen that Keegan was not his biological brother, just a liar like his kin.

After he'd divorced John's mother, Bryce had remarried a wealthy socialite with twin boys who were now in their late teens, whom Bryce doted on, by all accounts. *How does it feel to be replaced?* he wanted to ask John. *To feel like your dad chose another family he liked better?* Keegan knew the answer all too well.

"It wasn't an accident," Keegan said through gritted teeth. "Someone pushed them over."

Mitch fixed him with a puzzled stare. "Now, who exactly would do that?"

Keegan let his gaze roam over Mitch and Regina before landing on his father. "The same person who doesn't want Tracy to remember that he or she is a murderer."

"I'm not going back to the hospital," Tracy announced after she'd gone over the whole incident for what seemed like the millionth time. She sat on a hard chair in Bryce's neat-as-a-pin office, Keegan next to her and Chief Larraby scribbling notes. A certificate on the wall commemorated the day Bryce had been sworn in the year before as mayor of Copper Creek. On the walls were a dozen photos of Bryce posed next to various visitors, one showing him accepting some sort of certificate from a Scout troop. A cut-glass bowl of candy canes occupied a corner of his desk, no doubt for handing out to the youngest visitors. Bryce Larraby didn't miss a trick, she thought.

At the moment he, Mitch and Regina waited outside for their turns, sitting apart to prevent them from sharing stories, she imagined. It might have been anyone who'd pushed over the stacks. Then again, it might have been one of those three sitting right there in the lobby. All were strong enough, and each had had time to sneak to the upper catwalk and heave over the top hay bales.

Might it have been an accident as Bryce Larraby said? Something cold slithered up her spine as her instincts told her Keegan was right. It hadn't been an accident. Someone had tried to kill her. Again. If only she could remember whom she'd seen that night in the office.

As the chief finally dismissed her, she heaved herself to her feet. Keegan took her elbow and steered her to the door. "Let's go. I've had enough of this place."

"Me, too."

Chief Larraby snapped his notebook closed. "Probably best for you both to stay away from the Mother Lode for a while."

Tracy shook her head. "Believe me, I'd prefer never to set foot here again, but I have a job to do and several horses to evaluate. I'm not going to let my clients down."

"And we've got horses to supply for the auction," Keegan said. "And I've been training my cutting horse for too long to skip out now."

"Do the smart thing for once, Keeg."

"Do your job, John," he fired back. "Catch the killer."

John spoke through gritted teeth. "I will, if there is one."

After the hay incident, Tracy was convinced her memories were true, even if she couldn't recall the specifics.

Someone had killed a woman.

And that someone was ready to do the same to her.

This time Tracy urged Keegan away before he could get any deeper into an argument with his brother, but the irritation still burned hot in Keegan's chest. As they strode through the lobby, Bryce got to his feet. "I'm very sorry about the accident, Miss Wilson," he called out. "We'll make sure nothing like this happens again."

Keegan stared at his father, the man's expression fraught with concern. Real or faked? Keegan realized he could not see Bryce Larraby as everyone else did. To him, he would always be the man who'd rejected Keegan, made his mother's life one of misery. He would never understand how Bryce had gotten three women to love him.

Tracy urged him out of the building with a soft tug at his sleeve. He followed and managed to get to the passenger door before she did, opening it for her.

"Thank you," she said.

He got in and cranked the engine. It was dark now, the twinkling Christmas lights strung across the front eaves of the horse center lending it a cheer he did not feel.

He realized Tracy was shivering. "Cold?" He didn't wait for an answer but grabbed a blanket from behind his seat and put it on her lap. She spread it out and nestled down underneath.

"It's late. I don't think it's wise to drive you up to your property."

"But…"

"Come with me to my family's ranch. Stay the night."

"My grandpa…"

"Isn't arriving until tomorrow, you said."

"I'll be all right in the cabin."

"Got plumbing?"

"Yes." She shot him an offended look. "It's an old camp-ground, and we have buildings and running water and everything."

"Electricity?"

She deflated a little. "Well, no. Haven't got the transformer repaired yet."

"Groceries laid up in case we get some snow? You said you're in the foothills. We usually get a dusting this time of year, you know."

"I do know. I did my research."

"Got phone service up there? I've been able to text from a few spots, but not make phone calls."

She fell into silence. He restrained his impulse to keep talking. Instead he grabbed a meat stick and unwrapped it, biting off a piece and chewing thoughtfully.

He knew she didn't want to get any more involved in the life of the Thorns than she was already. She kept her past close to the vest, and she had to be terrorized by what had just happened and worried sick about the future. Why did that mix draw him like a moth to a flame?

She was pretty and in trouble, a combination he'd encountered before, but there was something about Tracy that made her unlike any woman he'd ever met, something he could not put his finger on. It made him want to find out more about what made her tick and keep her close, but "close" was dicey, because it could lead to deeper attachments. He'd never encouraged those kinds of attachments because he loathed the thought of hurting a woman like his father had. He cleared his throat. Why on earth was he mentally running through all that now? "Plenty of room at the Gold Bar."

"Keegan…"

"I know. You don't want me involved. I'm giving you a ride because your car is wrecked and you can't drive. I'm offering up a night's sleep and a meal to someone who could use them. That's just good manners, and if there's one thing I've been taught, it's good manners."

"Let me guess. Your mama is a good teacher?"

"My mama is more like a trick roping master. She'll smile and rope you into something and make you think you tied the knots yourself."

She smiled and he sensed her resolve weakening.

"You can get to know my brothers better and Betsy, that's Ella's sister. She had a stroke when she was a kid and she's in a wheelchair but it's amazing the things Ella's helped her learn. Besides, I'm starved. They stopped refilling the hospital cookies once they figured out it was me eating them all. It's Friday, so Mama will be making fried chicken. There is no one on this planet who makes better fried chicken than Mama, though I'm partial to her lasagna, too. Something about the way she combines the cheeses, I think."

"All right," Tracy said. "I'm hungry, too, and you're killing me. Are you sure she won't mind an unexpected houseguest?"

"I am absolutely positive, but I'll text her so she'll know to set an extra place." He kicked up the speed. "Besides, I can show you the best cutting horse you've ever been privileged to clap eyes on. Trained her myself."

"Your modesty is impressive."

"I speak the truth and you oughta know since you're a bloodstock agent." He shot a look at her. "You any good?"

A sigh escaped her. "Oh, yeah," she said. "I'm the best there is." She leaned against the headrest, the sunlight gilding her profile. Heart-shaped face, full lips, narrow chin, framed by hair the color of summer wheat. Soft and strong at the same time.

His breath hitched up for a moment and a grin crept over him.

Just friends, Keegan. Just friends.

SEVEN

The Gold Bar Ranch was impressive even in the darkness. Moonlight revealed acres of grass, neatly tended fences, a lovely stable and corrals sprawled alongside a cozy ranch-style home framed in Christmas lights. Nearby was a barn, outlined in golden lights with beribboned pine boughs above each wide door.

"Mama loves lights, so a Christmas Eve wedding was just the ticket," Keegan said as they pulled in. "Took me and my brothers an entire day to string 'em. Surprised we didn't blow the whole transformer grid to the town. Usually don't light the barn, but that's where the wedding is going to take place, so we're going the extra mile."

The scent of wood smoke tickled her nose as the winter air cut right through her thin jacket. The belongings in her duffel bag were still custody of the police department until they finished cataloging everything. She'd only visited her property twice, enough to bring in a few changes of clothes, a bed for herself, one for her grandfather and an extra cot in the vain hope that she could get her little sister, Lily, to visit someday, if her mother would allow it. That was a foolish expense, but it comforted her to know that cot was there…ready and waiting. She'd intended to gather up supplies after her stop at the horse center.

She felt again the claw of fear as memories scratched at the edges of her mind, begging to be let in. Keegan put his hand on the small of her back, and she realized she'd stopped walking.

"Okay?" Keegan inquired.

With a nod, she continued up the sweeping gravel drive. "Yes." If it could be considered okay to narrowly avoid being murdered twice since she'd hit town.

He pushed open the door and the warmth and light issuing from the interior almost made her cry. With such a tight-knit family, all eyes would be on her. The thought shallowed her breathing and there she was again, a teenager with an ex-con father. All the attention, all the judgment. She'd learned to covet invisibility, flying under the radar, and this was just about the opposite of that. She wanted to crawl inside her shell and lug herself right back to the truck.

And do what?

She could not drive, not legally, for another three days. And though she would not admit it to Keegan, the thought of spending the night alone on her isolated property scared her. Then again, so did the thought of experiencing this cozy Christmas setting.

Last year, after the lung cancer had started to smother her father, he'd been too sick to leave his bed, so, for Christmas, she'd brought in a tiny, one-foot-tall pine tree. He could smell it, he'd said, even if he could hardly hold his head up.

Grief turned her feet to lead. Christmas this year without her father would be bad enough, but with everything that had happened… Her eyes stung with unshed tears.

Get yourself together, Tracy.

Keegan slung an arm around her shoulders and propelled her up the porch steps. "It's okay. They don't bite, except maybe for Owen, but Ella's smoothed some of his edges away."

She wanted to resist, but she was just so tired and her head throbbed like it had when she'd been kicked by the horse.

In the next moment she was escorted through the cozy sitting room, complete with ivy-trimmed fireplace in which some logs crackled. Then it was into the kitchen, where a silver-haired woman, trim and petite, pulled pieces of fried chicken from a pan and set them on an enormous platter. A porcelain nativity scene glistened on the sideboard, surrounded by fat, red Christmas candles, flickering merrily.

The woman turned and put down her tongs, her smile broad. "Well, here you are. Keegan messaged to say he was bringing you. How are you feeling? I'm Keegan's mother. Please call me Evie."

For one long moment Tracy wanted nothing more than to throw herself into the arms of this capable mother, a woman whose house glowed with Christmas cheer, who cooked fried chicken and welcomed strangers without a second thought.

Evie wrapped her in a fried-chicken-scented hug and Tracy closed her eyes, breathing hard. "I'm very sorry to intrude," she managed to say.

The man who must be Evie's husband looked up from setting the table. "Not at all. The last friend Keegan brought home for dinner was an orphaned jackrabbit, so we're thrilled to have a young lady instead."

"It was a very friendly jackrabbit," Keegan said.

"I'm Tom Thorn. Please sit down. You've had a long day."

He didn't know the half of it. If she really allowed herself to reconstruct the events of the past forty-eight hours, she'd no doubt fall apart at the seams.

Evie took a cow bell from the counter and clanged it. "Now they'll come running. Easier than yelling."

Two men came in from the fields, twins she guessed, though not identical. Both took off their hats and nodded to her.

"Jack," the taller one said, extending a hand. "Pleased to formally meet you." His voice was soft, shy almost. "Sorry my fiancée, Shannon, isn't here. She's got another week of her ER residency down south." The pride shone clearly in his smile.

"Owen," said the other, broader around the shoulders, with hair cut military short. He shook her hand, his own so big it almost engulfed hers completely. "We met, actually, but you were unconscious at the time." His look was intense but not unfriendly, his bearing military. A Marine, she remembered, proud that she had actually recalled some snippet of conversation. "I hope you are recovered from your accident, ma'am."

"Tracy. And yes, I'm just tired." She did not add the information she knew he wanted, making him ask.

"Did you remember what you saw at the horse center?"

The kitchen went silent before Evie clucked at her son. "Later, Owen. She said she's tired."

He didn't comment, but Tracy knew he was right to ask. It was the giant elephant in the room. Did she remember the face of the killer? Or the identity of the victim?

"I…I actually can't remember much about that night. Not yet."

He gave her a long look and she was sure he was weighing the possible ramifications of what she'd said. It was all too much, the tension simmering just under the surface of their polite demeanor. She was grateful when they settled into chairs around the table.

A small redheaded woman with a plethora of freckles joined them, wheeling in a lady who, Tracy presumed, had to be her sister. All four men stood as the redhead positioned the wheelchair at the table before kissing Owen and taking a seat in the chair he pulled out for her, next to Keegan's mother. Their formal cowboy manners made Tracy's heart throb. She'd never been treasured by a man except her father and grandfather, in his own gruff way. Did Ella know how blessed she was? As Ella shot an adoring look at Owen, cupping a hand over his cheek, Tracy decided that she did.

"I'm Ella," she said by way of introduction, looking at Tracy, "and this is my sister, Betsy. We don't actually live here at the moment—it just seems like we do."

"Soon enough we'll have our own place. Put an offer down last week." Pride shone on Owen's face. "A nice piece of land fifteen minutes from here. Got a house on it already with enough room for the three of us, but we'll expand as we need to."

Ella blushed and he kissed her on the forehead.

"Barrett phoned and said Shelby has a case of indigestion." Evie laughed. "I remember I had indigestion for nine months when I was expecting the twins."

"Owen's fault," Jack said.

Evie laughed. "Anyway, they won't be joining us for dinner tonight."

Tom prayed a simple prayer and the platter of chicken began its journey around the table, along with a pile of fluffy mashed potatoes and peas. She helped herself to the potatoes and peas and passed them along.

"You forgot your chicken," Keegan said, ready to grab a piece for her plate.

"No, thank you," she said. "It looks delicious but…"

"Oh, really, honey—there's plenty. Don't feel shy," Evie said.

Tracy felt her cheeks burn as they all looked curiously at her. "I'm… I don't want to be rude, but I'm a vegetarian."

There were several round-eyed looks, the roundest from Keegan. "You don't eat meat?"

"No."

"Like…ever?"

"Not since I was ten."

"Well, how are you still upright?" His look was so incredulous she giggled while Evie scolded him.

"Keegan Thorn. What she eats is her business and you're not to call attention to it."

"Yes, ma'am," he said, but his look was still befuddled.

"Not to worry, Tracy," Evie said. "Owen's Marine friend stayed with us for two months and he was a vegan. I had to read up on that one. Vegetarian fare is easy." She got to her feet and returned with a bowl of plastic-wrapped three-bean salad. "Here you go. Protein."

"You didn't have to…"

She waved an airy hand. "I made some for church. I know my way around a bean."

"That she does," Tom said.

"And Christmas cookies," Keegan added. "Did you make some with the gumdrops in them?"

"You mean another batch, since you raided them before they even cooled?" Evie eyed him with an arched brow.

"I didn't eat them by myself. Ella and Owen helped."

Owen laughed. "We had to content ourselves with the crumbs you left behind."

After the laughter died away, they dug into their meals and Tracy felt some strength return as her appetite fired to life. The mashed potatoes were creamy and glistening with melted butter, and the vinegary bean salad made her taste buds sing.

The conversation shifted between ranch details, lively discussions about Keegan's cutting horse, and the new mares the ranch had just received to train and board for clients. One thousand acres and sixty horses made for a lot of chatter. She noticed that Ella was eyeing her curiously over the top of her glass of iced tea.

Tracy began to squirm, as she always did when attention was riveted on her. As she took a sip of iced tea, Ella snapped her fingers. "Tracy Wilson. I finally figured it out."

"Figured…what out?"

"I know you."

"You do? But I don't remember meeting you."

Ella raised an eyebrow, looking as though she were putting together an intricate puzzle in her mind.

Tracy's stomach jumped. What had Ella remembered? And what else had Tracy forgotten?

Keegan cocked his head at Ella. "Did you two meet sometime?"

"Yes and no."

Tracy looked from Ella to Keegan, a fearful sheen in her eyes that made Keegan's breath catch. "Let's have it, Ella."

She pulled her phone from her pocket and thumbed the screen. "A month ago you sent me an email. My full name is Joella Cahill, so you didn't put the names together."

"Joella Cahill?" Tracy toyed with her napkin. "The farrier. Of course. I contacted you because I was coming to Copper Creek for the horse show and you are a well-respected farrier."

"Yes, she is," Owen said. "The best."

Ella blushed. "You asked me if I would take a look at

a few horses for you, give my evaluation on their hoof health."

Tracy nodded, relieved. "I make it a point to seek out experts whenever I can. I know the basics, but a good farrier can tell a horse's whole life history from their hooves, it seems to me." She frowned as a detail snapped into place. "We were going to meet."

"Tomorrow, at the Mother Lode," Ella said. "You said you'd confirm a time the day before, but I didn't hear back."

Keegan pushed back in his chair. "Her plans were changed without her consent." He felt the dark rage slither around in his belly again.

"I'm sorry. I lost my phone, or I would have remembered when I checked my calendar."

"What about the vet?" Ella asked.

Tracy shook her head. "What vet?"

Ella turned the phone around so they could both see. "There was supposed to be a third person at our meeting. A veterinarian." Her coppery brows drew together. "A woman, Dr. Nan Ridley. I'd never worked with her before, but you said in your message she was on staff at the Mother Lode for the Silver Spurs show."

"That's right. I can't think why I didn't remember earlier. My memory is like Swiss cheese since the accident."

Keegan had the search started before either of his brothers could pull out their phones. He pulled up the website for the Yuletide Silver Spurs Horse Show and selected the tab marked Staff. "I see Mitch Arnold here, a stable manager. Regina Parker, a publicity person. And some miscellaneous people. Hang on. The staff veterinarian is a guy named Hal Severin, not Nan Ridley."

"Maybe I made a mistake in my email." Tracy's brow creased. "But I must have contacted Nan if I was setting up a meeting." She rubbed her forehead. "I wish I had my phone, or my laptop. It's up at the property."

Owen pushed his phone in front of her. "I did an internet search. There is a local vet named Nan Ridley in Parkersville, about fifteen miles south of us. Here's her picture."

Tracy angled the phone to the light. The face jarred something to life. Crying out, she dropped it onto the table with a clatter, her skin pale as moonlight.

Everyone leaned in, but Tracy turned her horrified gaze on Keegan. A dark realization clouded the brilliant hazel of her eyes.

"I remembered just now. I've seen her before. That's... I think that's the woman I saw being murdered."

EIGHT

Nan Ridley peered back at Keegan from the phone screen. The long dark hair, the brown eyes, full mouth. Snatches of that night came back in flickering filmstrip moments, and he recalled the terror evident on Tracy's face when he'd first seen her heading into the train station. Maybe she was wrong about Nan, about what she'd seen, but he had the dreadful sensation that he was looking at the smiling photo of a dead woman.

Tracy pushed back from the table and stumbled away, would have fallen if Keegan hadn't caught her around the waist and steered her into a stuffed chair by the fireplace in the sitting room. The others followed, uncertain what to do. She sat there shivering. Evie brought her a blanket, which Keegan arranged over her lap, but it did not seem to warm her.

Owen stepped into the kitchen to call the police station.

Keegan knelt next to her and put a hand on her knee. "You remember?"

"I'm so afraid, Keegan. I...saw her murdered." Her breaths came in little panicked bursts. "I wish with everything inside me that I was wrong. I still can't bring up the details of the killer's face."

"You will," he said. "Give yourself time."

"Time?" Her teeth chattered. "Time for the killer to find me before I can remember?" Hysteria crept into her voice and she bit her lip, struggling for control.

"No one is going to hurt you." He reached for her shaking fingers, rolling them in his. "I won't let them."

She swallowed hard and clamped her jaws together.

Evie brought in a steaming mug and pressed it into her grasp. "Decaf. Once you're warmed up, you can take a hot shower and tumble right into bed. You can use Keegan's room and he can bunk with Jackie."

Jack rolled his eyes. "Great. I'll be up when he needs his midnight snack."

"If you're nice, I'll make you one, too. My bologna, cheese and pickles sandwich is legendary." He winked at Tracy as he shot the comeback at his brother. That garnered a tiny quirk of a smile from her.

He sat close, one ear on the conversation taking place in the fringes of the room. His family gathered in the firelight and set about their amateur sleuthing. Owen was jotting notes on a yellow pad while Jack, Ella and Tom hunted for information about Nan Ridley on their phones.

His mom refilled Tracy's mug when her coffee went cold and gave her shoulder a squeeze. "They're not exactly private eyes," she said. "But they are determined as dogs on a scent when they're trying to help a friend. I'll go get some clean sheets on the bed for you."

The lamplight teased out gold flecks in Tracy's hair, along with a gleam of moisture in her eyes.

"You have an amazing family," she whispered to Keegan.

"Yeah," he said. "Amazing they took me in, my biological roots are so twisted. I was a loud-mouthed, thrill-seeking kid who nearly ate them out of house and home. Dunno why they decided to love me." He'd been trying for a joke. She did not smile.

"Maybe because you let them," she said. The comment came out almost absently as she looked into the dancing flames in the fireplace.

He straightened, getting to his feet and pacing a bit, pretending to examine something outside the window as her words ricocheted inside. The Thorns loved him, and he loved them. But when Keegan stood still long enough, it occurred to him that he did not allow anyone else to do so. The women he dated, the people he met. No big deal, anyway, was it? He had a houseful of brothers and soon-to-be sisters-in-law. They filled up the places in his heart left empty by his pathetic excuse for a father and those he had lost—his mother, and Barrett's first wife, Bree, who had been closer than a sister to him.

"I'm hungry," he said to Tracy. "Can I get you anything?"

She shot him a wondering look. "But we just ate."

"Didn't have dessert. Mama baked a gingerbread cake, which she hid, but I know where she put it."

"No, you don't," his mother said as she returned. "I found an even better hiding spot."

"Good thing for me, you're only four feet and change, so I never have to look in the high places." He loved her grin that meant she enjoyed the game as much as he did. He pressed a kiss to her temple. When they'd first adopted him after being his unofficial guardians for years, he'd been so angry he could not accept love from anyone, so her cooking had been the bridge between them. Everything she made was done with love, and he could taste it in each bite. He hugged her, gathering close the small woman with the biggest heart in the world.

"Okay," Owen said suddenly. "I found Nan Ridley's office phone number. My call went straight to voice mail. I asked her to return the call as soon as she could."

Tom glanced up from his laptop. "She's got a blog, too, called Horsing Around, but she hasn't posted anything to it since earlier this week."

"Earlier this week," Tracy echoed.

"Tuesday," he said, "to be exact."

Keegan followed the thought. He'd found Tracy at the train station Wednesday night. Perhaps there had been no more blog posts from Nan because she was no longer alive.

The knock at the door made Tracy jump. Keegan opened it to find John, in civilian clothes. He preferred seeing his half brother in uniform—it reinforced that they were completely different. Seeing him in jeans and a windbreaker reminded Keegan that their biological link could not be wished away. John shared his dark hair, the strong chin, lanky build and big hands, and Keegan didn't enjoy the reminder of their biological link.

John took off his baseball cap and sat in the chair Evie offered as she bustled back in with another cup of coffee. He took it with a grateful nod and a "Thank you, ma'am" before he turned his attention to Tracy.

She sucked in a breath. "Did you find out anything, Chief?"

"There's simply no way to tell if the bales were knocked over or fell of their own accord." Keegan started to interrupt, but John held up a palm. "My officers and I have interviewed everybody on site, and we got nothing."

Keegan restrained a sarcastic remark. "You need to investigate a woman, a veterinarian named Nan Ridley."

"Why, may I ask?" John's voice was tight.

Tracy explained. "She was the staff veterinarian for the Yuletide Silver Spurs Horse Show. I made arrangements via email to meet her and Ella Cahill. I...I think she was the woman I saw being murdered."

John's eyes narrowed a fraction after Ella showed him the email from Tracy.

"I might have more info, if I could figure out where my phone went."

John drew a plastic bag from his pocket. "It's here. We retrieved it from the office at the horse center." He handed her a duffel bag. "Your clothes and Smith & Wesson."

Tracy leaped to her feet. "My phone must have fallen out when I ran. That proves I was there."

John's expression didn't change. "I'm sorry, but it only proves your phone was there. It was on the counter, as if someone left it there for the lost and found."

"But my messages. Maybe there're more from Nan."

John handed it to her and she used Owen's cord to plug it in. The faint glow as the phone powered on reflected the hope on her face. She tapped away at the screen. "Here, here's the email from Nan, confirming our meeting for tomorrow." Keegan watched as her face clouded in disbelief. "Wait. There's a follow-up." She read from the screen. "'I'm sorry I'm unable to make our meeting. I've been offered another opportunity, so I am headed to Phoenix for a couple of months. I am sure the new vet at the Mother Lode will be able to help you.'"

The room went dead quiet.

Tracy groaned and closed her eyes. "But I was so sure what I saw."

"Someone could be sending the emails using Nan's phone," Jack said.

John cleared his throat. "I'll corroborate, check with her office and at the Mother Lode."

Keegan paced around the small room. "What about the shooting? Bullets? Anything?"

"We've looked at all of it, but nothing points back to the horse center."

"Well, what other reason would there be for someone to shoot at the Jeep and nearly kill us?"

John stood and put down his coffee, squaring up with Keegan. "You got into a little scrap the day of the crash, I hear. Neglected to mention it to me, didn't you?"

"A scrap?" Keegan stared until a memory jolted him. "Oh, you mean the guy at the gas station? Sonny B? I forgot all about that. He has a beef with me and tried to rough me up a little."

Evie clutched the towel she was holding. "Oh, Keegan. Not that gang again?"

He offered his mom a smile, though he was seething at John, who he was sure was enjoying upsetting his mother. "No big deal, Mama. Just some bad blood left over from when I considered patching into the Aces." He explained for Tracy. "I considered joining up with their gang. Fortunately, I came to my senses before it was too late."

"More like we rescued you from your own lunacy," Owen said.

He laughed. "True. In any case, I got into plenty of trouble during my probationary phase. Sonny B was with a rival gang of ours, the East Siders, and he tried to teach me his rules. I'm not a good rule follower."

"That's an understatement," Jack muttered.

John half smiled. "Funny how these things come back to plague us, huh? Sins of the past?"

Keegan faced him. "Sonny B came at me, threw the first punch. I defended myself. I left. He left. That was it. Just a small scuffle, not my first and probably not my last."

John's lip quirked. "Are you sure he didn't follow you to the train station? Decide to take out you and your girl all in one? Nice revenge move that would get him some cred with his East Siders buddies, wouldn't it?"

Keegan's muscles went wire taut. "That's ridiculous."

He shrugged. "My job is to chase down all the possibilities, even if they sound ridiculous to you."

The breath turned hot in Keegan's lungs, burning him from the inside out. "You can't run this investigation, John. You're too anxious to pin it on me."

"You're right, for once. I would love to pin something on you."

They stood face-to-face, hands fisted, Owen and Jack stepping closer to intervene.

"Gentlemen," his father said, voice low and hard. "I will not have any violence in this house. Am I clear?"

Neither Keegan nor John backed down. Finally, after an endless moment, John shifted his gaze to Tom. "I'm handling the shooting investigation and helping the Copper Creek cops with the rest, since it's not my jurisdiction."

"Why doesn't that make me feel any better?" Keegan muttered.

John looked at Tracy. "Keep me apprised of your living situation and contacts, et cetera. I'll have follow-up questions after I talk to Nan Ridley. I'll have the cops talk to the people at the horse center about her employment."

"Dad will be able to tell them." Keegan felt the slam of his heartbeat against his ribs. "He knows every detail of what goes on at his place."

John didn't answer. He nodded to Evie. "Thank you for the coffee. I'll be in touch soon."

When John left, Keegan paced a few more circles around the family room as he tried to walk off the encounter with his half brother. "This is just a little too neat, isn't it? Nan suddenly leaving town?"

He shouldn't have said it aloud. Tracy dropped her head. "I have a terrible feeling. I don't want to be right, but I'm... I'm afraid she's dead, no matter what the email said."

He went to her and touched her shoulder. "We'll figure it out."

"The police…" she started.

"We won't get in their way, but we can do a little sleuthing on our own." His brothers answered with a nod.

"No, absolutely not," Tracy said. "You have weddings to plan, and this isn't your problem." She got to her feet, a little unsteadily, appealing to his mother. "Mrs. Thorn, if I could take you up on that offer to spend the night, I would be very grateful. Tomorrow, I'll go up to my property." She left the rest unspoken. *And take care of my problems by myself.*

"Of course—" Evie gestured "—follow me. I'll show you to your room."

After they left, Keegan's brothers stared at him.

"You're not gonna leave this to the police, are you?" Owen demanded.

"Since when have I ever walked away from trouble?" He forced a grin, but for once the glib remark didn't ring true in his heart.

Trouble, he felt deep down, was speeding like an arrowhead, straight for Tracy Wilson.

Evie led Tracy to a small room with a bed and dresser crammed into the corner. The old wood floor showed scuff marks from years of cowboy boots walking across it, and the mirror atop the dresser was crowded with taped-on photos. While Evie rounded up towels and an extra blanket, Tracy perused the photos. They were striking black-and-whites, horse pictures mostly, some family shots, one of Keegan as a much younger boy being hoisted into the air by the three Thorn boys, all of them smiling.

Two of the pictures stood out, also black-and-whites, one of a woman, who had to be his mother, clutching a very young Keegan to her side, lips parted and long hair thrown back as if she'd been caught in a laugh. Keegan was smiling, too, not in the joking, wisecracker way, but in the wide, innocent smile of a child who was loved and had not yet encountered a world full of trouble.

Evie came close. "Keegan's mother. She came to live with us when Keegan was ten, worked on the ranch. She passed from breast cancer when he was almost sixteen, and we adopted him." Evie smiled. "She was a spunky lady with a heart of gold. Naive, too. She believed every word Bryce told her. Never suspected he was married."

Tracy examined the other picture. A different woman, lovely, shooting a look at the camera that was puzzled, innocent. "Who's this?"

Evie sighed. "Barrett's first wife, Bree. She was like a sister to Keegan. She could tell him things that he wouldn't hear from me." Evie carefully detached the photo. On the back was a scripture jotted in smeared ink pen. *"Bear ye one another's burdens, and so fulfill the law of Christ. Galatians 6:2."*

"When things were particularly bad, he threw away all the other pictures of her, but he kept this one."

"Did they…? Did she and Barrett divorce?"

"No. She was killed by a drunk driver." Evie blew out a breath. "We are so thrilled that Barrett found Shelby, and excited about the baby, but none of us will ever forget Bree, especially Keegan."

Tracy was startled when Evie folded her into a hug. "Sleep well, Tracy. Give a shout if there's anything you need. I'll be praying for you."

Tracy thanked her and, as Evie closed the door, she was overwhelmed by an urge to phone her mother, to grab hold of some maternal warmth. But it would do no good. Her mother would make polite small talk, cold and impersonal, the wall that had sprung up between them the moment Tracy had decided to live with her father after his release from prison still firmly in place.

How can you take his side, after everything I've done for you? He's a criminal. He ruined this family.

I love you both, but he needs me more now. He's sick.

She remembered the stricken look on her mother's face, as if she'd slapped her.

Make your choice, Tracy, but you'd better be sure you can accept the consequences. If you go live with him, I don't want you at my home or near your sister. She's too young, and I don't want her around a criminal.

Tracy looked again at the Bible verse on the back of Bree's picture. Bearing one another's burdens sometimes came at a cost. The consequences of choosing to bear her father's had been agonizing. She'd lost her mother and her sister.

Keegan was certainly eager to bear her burdens—for a woman he'd only just met—but he was completely closed off to his own half brother. It was totally understandable, in Tracy's book. Betrayal served up by strangers or even friends was so much easier to forgive than that doled out by kin. She could forgive him for it, unless, she thought with a flip of her stomach, he was using her situation to punish the family that had wronged him.

Tomorrow, she decided. Tomorrow she would find another way to get up to her property. She squeezed her hands together, eyes shut tight, and once again asked the Lord to heal her fractured family.

NINE

Keegan awoke from a restless night. He'd tossed and turned until Jack growled out the suggestion that he go bunk on the living room sofa. He'd tried, with no better success, in spite of the pine-scented coziness and twinkling Christmas lights his mother insisted stay on all night long.

Now, as the black sky turned to slate gray, he forked down flakes of hay into the bed of his truck and drove them to feed the north pasture horses. That was followed by a vigorous mucking out of the stalls and a text to Ella to have her reshoe Starlight, a placid gelding they were boarding while his owners were in Europe.

As the sun broke through, gilding the distant hillside, he saddled Outlaw and took him into the western pasture, where they grazed a herd of cattle. Being with the big sorrel horse soothed him, steadied the thrumming of his pulse. Outlaw's ears pricked as they neared the cattle and Keegan felt the same flicker of enthusiasm. He stroked his sleek neck. "Want to do your thing, Outlaw?"

He led the horse into the pasture and the cows bunched nervously, eyeing Keegan and Outlaw. He guided Outlaw into the middle of the herd, cutting it in two, and then he chose his animal, a robust black bull calf. Their communication was spot-on, as it always was. Keegan needed only to guide, suggest with a slight pressure in his knees, a touch of his hand, and Outlaw went to work, edging back and forth, contorting in ways that defied the laws of nature for a two-thousand-pound animal, until the calf was neatly separated from the herd.

"That a boy," Keegan said, scrubbing his fingers along Outlaw's neck. "That's gonna earn you another championship at the Yuletide show."

When the calf had scampered back to his mother, Keegan let himself out the gate and secured it behind him, surprised to see Tracy watching him.

She wore a pair of jeans rolled up at the ankles and a soft green sweatshirt he suspected had been borrowed from one of his soon-to-be sisters-in-law.

"That's a beautiful quarter horse."

"Yes, he is."

She laughed. "You both have the same cocky attitude."

"That's a winning attitude, ma'am."

"Right. Well, winning is all about hard work, in my book."

"Mine, too."

Her smile dimmed. "Anyway, I came to tell you that if you can drop me in town, I'll purchase some supplies and my grandpa will meet me there. There's no need for you to drive me up to the mountains."

Disappointment licked his insides. Was that it? Tracy would sequester herself in the foothills and he'd have no more reason to be in her life? Why should it matter? He hadn't even known her for a week. But for some reason it did matter, the thought of her leaving. It mattered very much, but he could think of no way to avoid it. Yet. He'd stall for time until he cobbled together a better plan.

He held out a palm. "Want a ride back to the house?"

She hesitated only a moment before she took his hand

and he swung her up behind him. She held on to the saddle's cantle and kept her legs far forward to avoid touching Outlaw's flanks, a sensitive area on any horse.

"You really do know your horses, don't you?"

She laughed, the sound small and silvery, the smell of her shampoo enticing. "Did you think I was lying?"

"Nah, just figured maybe exaggerating a little."

"Horses are my life. That's why my grandpa and I are starting up a family horse camp. Someday, when we can get all the details worked out."

By "details," he suspected she meant the finances. "Great idea."

"It was my father's dream. He helped while… I mean, while he was in prison, some of the inmates with expertise were allowed to go work at a horse camp for disabled vets."

He felt a whisper of tension from behind him. "What was your dad in for? That's probably nosy, right? So if you don't want to answer…"

"He assaulted his business partner. They ran a trucking business together and his partner was stealing money. Dad couldn't prove it, but he went to confront the man and it turned violent. Dad went to jail and the company folded. My mom…she divorced him, cut off any contact. Dad regretted his actions, asked forgiveness when he was re-leased, but he didn't find it from many people."

"Except you. That must have meant a lot to him."

"He got out of prison, but by then he was sick with lung cancer. I went to live with him when I was a high school senior, took care of him until he died. Finished up my schooling, somehow."

"That must have been hard."

"Yeah. My classmates were…unkind. They said all manner of things about my father…and me. Ever since, I prefer to be on my own."

"Is that why there's no boyfriend or fiancé?"

She laughed, and he realized he'd been extremely nosy once again.

"You do say what's on your mind, don't you?"

"Sorry," he said, but he hoped she'd answer in spite of his rudeness.

"I learned that people's love and loyalty can change like the wind. My friends, my community, even my mother's love for my dad." She sighed. "It's just easier to go it alone."

He wanted to turn around and hold her close and show her he understood. Completely. "I hear you. My half brother couldn't slander my mother's reputation enough. Said she was a gold digger for insisting on a paternity test. She only did it after she feared she wasn't going to survive the cancer. Wanted me to have something." He cleared his throat. "I wouldn't take any of my so-called father's money anyway. My mother put what little was left after expenses in the bank, but that's gonna go to my nieces or nephews. I don't need his money. It was never about that."

It was about being acknowledged as something other than a mistake. Inexplicably, he felt moisture building behind his eyelids and he shook away his own idiocy.

"So that's why there's no girlfriend? No fiancée?" she teased. He owed her an answer, and he found it was an honest one, rather than his usual flippancy.

"I enjoy the company of women, as friends. Anything more is too risky." He shrugged. "I've met some amazing women in my life, and the last thing I'd want to do is betray one like my father did to my mother." He'd never before told anyone his fear about emulating Bryce. His own candor surprised him.

"What a pair we are, Keegan. I don't trust people and you don't trust yourself."

"Guess we're better off alone." He'd never been sad about the idea until that very moment.

He felt a gentle pressure as she laid her head between his shoulder blades. "My dad always said forgiving the living is hard, but forgiving the dead's even harder. He went to his grave believing my mother hated him, and part of him felt he deserved it. He didn't. He tried so hard to make amends."

Keegan's father and half brother had never so much as lifted a finger to make amends. Or had they and he'd just never let them?

More idiocy. Annoyed with himself, he let Outlaw pick up the pace, his own drive to end the conversation nearly overwhelming him. Why did her attitude remind him of Bree's?

Bear one another's burdens... Bree would have said it, smiled and poked a finger into his chest.

And he would, for anyone else but his half brother and biological father. Anyone else but them. Surely God would understand why. They didn't care about the harm they'd caused, the burden he carried that steered him away from spectacular women like Tracy.

It's safer that way. You get half your genes from a lousy excuse for a husband.

He put the thoughts away as he led Outlaw back to the Gold Bar stables.

Tracy inhaled the rich scent of coffee that drifted along the streets of Gold Bar.

"At least let me buy you a cup of coffee while you wait for your grandfather." Keegan held the door of the Sunrise Café for her, and she found herself agreeing. She knew it would be best to speedily walk out of Keegan's life, figure out what to do on her own, but the blue eyes, the warm smile, his touch on her wrist, stopped her. What could one cup of coffee hurt? Even people who chose to go it alone needed company occasionally.

It was like stepping back in time as she followed Keegan across the checkerboard-tiled floor past an aluminum Christmas tree crowded with presents underneath for the staff. The pie case was jammed with holiday favorites: pecan, pumpkin, eggnog custard.

Her phone vibrated as she slid behind him into a booth. "Someone is calling. I don't recognize the number." She answered. "Hello?"

There was a click as someone disconnected. She forced down a sense of fear. "Wrong number?"

Keegan frowned. "Probably."

Tracy sipped her black coffee, puzzling, as Keegan added two creams and a healthy dose of sugar to his mug. She kept an eye on the door for her grandfather.

"What's he look like?" Keegan asked. "Did you get your gorgeous looks from him?"

She laughed, cheeks warm. Gorgeous? It sounded like a line she'd heard before, but for some reason Keegan said it with such sincerity that the compliment wasn't easily deflected. "He's big, tough and grumpy—what you'd expect from an old-school sheep rancher—but he's a teddy bear inside."

Keegan laughed. "No doubt."

The café was suddenly filled with a group of ranch hands, a half dozen men and women, some in jeans, others in coveralls and work boots. She recognized Mitch with his arm around Regina. Bryce Larraby poked his head through the double doors.

"Coffee's on me for everyone, Meg," he called to the cashier. "These folks have been working their fingers to the bone." His gaze traveled over the booths and she thought he started a bit when he caught sight of her and Keegan. He smiled and nodded at them before he headed back out the door. The noise of the crowd ebbed and flowed, and she noticed one bearded man staring at her. He whispered to his friend and jerked a chin in her direction, causing her face to go from warm to hot.

"That's her," he heard the man say. "Causing trouble for Bryce. Probably looking for a payout."

Keegan half rose, fury pinching his mouth.

"Don't," she said, clamping a hand on his forearm. "Please."

He allowed himself to be pulled to his seat, but he kept up a hostile gaze until the man looked away.

Tracy pushed out a breath. "I'm going to the ladies' room. Keep an eye out for my grandfather, okay?"

Keegan nodded. She leaned close and put her lips to his ear. "Keegan, don't say anything to those men. It will just make things worse. They're loyal to Bryce Larraby. There's nothing wrong with that."

"There's plenty wrong with that," Keegan muttered, but he kept his seat as she edged out of the booth.

Scooting to the back of the crowd, she hurried to the ladies' room, letting herself into a stall and standing there, breath tight.

They think...they all think that I made the whole thing up to extort money. She pressed her forehead to the cool metal door of the stall. If she could just remember the face of the killer, some small detail...

She closed her eyes, re-creating the darkened office at the Mother Lode center. An impression of the killer pressed into her senses, chilling her bones, teasing her skin into goose bumps. Someone tall, broad-shouldered, face cloaked in shadows, but enough light for her to see...what?

Long hair? Was the killer a woman? Or was her mind mixing up the details of the killer and victim?

Think. You've got to think.

Nothing emerged in her memory but her panicked flight, the broken ornament, running into Keegan at the train station...

And then she flashed on her pulling her father's gun from her pocket and firing, Keegan emerging from the hole in the floor, unharmed but irate.

What else you got in those pockets? A Winchester? Nunchucks?

A grin lit her face. "So that's why he calls me Pockets," she murmured. It wasn't much progress but at least she'd remembered another small thing.

She was about to fling the stall door open when she heard footsteps on the tile. No need to face down any more hostile strangers. She'd wait until the other occupant was safely locked in a stall before she exited.

But she heard another sound instead: the scrape of a heavy object being pulled along the floor.

Prickles erupted along her skin as she caught the smell of something poisonous, something deadly.

TEN

Keegan sat drinking coffee and listening to Frank Sinatra croon out Christmas carols while the stable workers grabbed their mugs and crowded into the available tables.

Mitch strolled past with Regina tucked into the crook of his arm, though she was almost taller than the bull breeder. Mitch smiled, but Regina did not.

"Morning," Mitch said.

He returned the greeting. "Got a question for you."

"You're full of them, aren't you?" Regina snapped.

He worked to keep his tone level. "People with nothing to hide don't mind a few questions."

Her eyes flashed. "Bryce has nothing to hide, and you've caused him crazy amounts of trouble with your accusations that someone was murdered. You just want to punish him because of something that happened when you were a kid. Grow up, Keegan. Lots of people have busted-up families. Isn't that right, Mitch?"

Mitch's mouth quirked in irritation. "For sure. My old man thought he was some kind of military hero and his family was a platoon to be ordered around. Regina here... well, you don't even know your daddy, now do you?"

Regina shrugged. "Bryce has been like a dad to me. He's a great man."

Keegan ground his teeth and stared back at her. "This isn't because he's my father."

"Isn't it?"

Mitch squeezed Regina's shoulders and gave a forced smile. "Bryce is fine, baby. He can handle it. Everything's on track for the show. A question or two won't make a difference."

Keegan asked quickly while she took a breath to respond. "Who's Nan Ridley?"

Regina's mouth snapped closed, as if she'd been surprised by the question.

"Nan?" Mitch squinted in thought. "Oh, wait. She was supposed to be the vet at the horse show. Seemed eager to be there but got a better offer. Quit, I heard."

"When?"

"Last week sometime, but Bryce would know the exact date. Why are you asking about her?"

Keegan ignored Mitch's question. "Did you know her?"

Regina shrugged. "Yeah. Not well. Our paths didn't cross that often and she was kinda snooty."

Mitch laughed. "You think every female is kinda snooty, especially when they spend time chatting with me."

Regina flushed. "Maybe if you didn't go out of your way to be so charming to the ladies."

He squeezed her close and pressed a kiss to her cheek. "It's cute that you're jealous."

"What did you talk about with her?" Keegan asked Mitch.

"Business. The care and feeding of bucking bulls. She wanted to be sure I was treating them well. I told her, 'Honey, these animals are my bread and butter. They get treated better than my women.'" He laughed. Keegan noticed Regina did not.

"Anyway, I only spoke to her a couple of times. Seemed

nice, efficient in an uptight sort of city-girl way. That's all I know about Nan, but you could ask around." He jutted a chin at the stable workers, many of whom were obviously listening to the whole conversation. "But I wouldn't expect a lot of cooperation if I were you." His tone turned steely and he leaned closer. "Unlike you, they've all got a lot of respect for Bryce." He flashed another smile. "Enjoy your coffee."

The room suddenly felt hot, suffocating, filled with people who worshipped Bryce Larraby as some sort of hero. The injustice of it burned. Bryce was a man who had ensnared a vulnerable young woman, gotten her pregnant and refused to acknowledge his offspring until he was legally forced to. And that was all he'd ever done. To date, Bryce had never called him son, only John and his stepsons, Marie's twins. Why were they worthy of acknowledgment and he was not?

You wouldn't want it anyway, not from that man. He had a father in Tom Thorn and an amazing mother, parents who were worthier by far than his own blood. So why did it matter what kind of man he was biologically linked to? And if it didn't matter…why did he let it influence his relationships? All of a sudden, he was unable to sit still for another moment.

He paid for the coffee and headed for the door, figuring he could watch for both Tracy and her grandfather if he stood just outside. The December sunshine blinded him for a moment, and someone bumped into him. He was about to apologize for the contact, though it wasn't his fault, when he recognized the short, stocky man with the long ponytail snaking out from under a bandanna, the tattooed biceps bulging out of a sleeveless leather vest.

"Hello, Keegan," Sonny B said.

Keegan bit back a groan. His day was heading right down the sewer. "Sonny, I don't want trouble."

"Since when?"

Since I met Tracy Wilson. He was surprised at the thought. Until recently he would not have shied away from trouble, and he might have even welcomed it. But now... well, he had other concerns, trying to give Tracy back the life she deserved. "Look, man, I don't have a beef with you anymore."

"Well, maybe I got a beef with you, tough guy." His fists went up.

Keegan raised his reflexively. "I don't want to be a part of this. Not now."

Sonny's eyes formed slits. "You embarrassed me in front of my boys. Made me look foolish."

That wasn't hard to do, he thought but managed to keep the words inside. "That was a long time ago."

"Not long enough." Sonny threw a punch, which Keegan easily ducked. People began to gather on the sidewalk, including an older man with a bald head and a wide set of shoulders filling out a worn flannel shirt.

"Seriously, man, I don't have time for this right now."

Sonny glared. "Well, you're gonna make time, whether you like it or not."

Someone pushed past the gathered gawkers—his brother Jack.

He eyed Sonny B like a bucking horse. "Keeg? You need a wingman?"

Keegan kept his fists up. "I was trying to explain to this guy that I'm not interested in trouble."

Keegan knew his brother better than anyone alive and only he could detect the well-hidden surprise in Jack's face. "That sounds like mighty good sense to me." Jack jutted a chin at Sonny B. "You got no reason to stay. Beat it."

"Why should I?"

Jack smiled. "It's almost Christmas."

"Don't care. I can mess up your brother on a holiday, no sweat on me."

Jack's smile vanished. "All right. How about this one? Because my other two brothers are across the street at the hardware store, and they're both stronger than I am and a good sight meaner."

Sonny took in Jack's height and then his gaze shifted to Keegan. "Maybe I got some brothers of my own. I can call 'em up right now."

Keegan was about to answer when he heard a sound that chilled his blood—a woman's scream coming from the back of the coffee shop, a woman he knew in his gut was Tracy.

Almost at the same moment the fire alarm began to blare. He looked at Jack.

"I'll go around the back!" Jack shouted as Keegan charged into the exiting diners, desperate to get to Tracy.

Tracy's scream was drowned out by the shrilling fire alarm. She fumbled for her phone as she smelled the tang of something familiar: the harsh scent of bleach and a pungent ammonia odor. Bleach plus ammonia equaled death. It must be a mistake. No one would be mixing those two deadly elements unless they had murder on their mind.

She tried to peer through the crack in the stall door to be sure the intruder was gone, but she did not have a good sight line. The alarm continued to bleat. Whoever was trying to poison her had set it off as a diversion. People would be leaving the building, unaware of her plight.

As the toxic fumes began to fill the air, she pulled the neck of her sweater over her mouth to keep from breathing in the poison. Her eyes were already watering, vision blurring and lungs burning as the chemicals mixed together to form chloramine. There wasn't much time.

Call later, get out now.

She ripped open the stall door, ushering in a wave of chemicals that made her gag. The intruder had dumped the trash can and upended the two bottles in the container to allow the contents to begin their deadly work. He or she must have had something over their nose and mouth.

Tracy raced to the bathroom door and tugged. It didn't budge. Panicked, she yanked on it for several seconds until she realized the wooden doorstop had been jammed under the door and it was hopelessly stuck. Terror nearly brought her to the floor. She grabbed the phone from her pocket and tried to dial, to call Keegan, the police, but her hands were trembling badly and her vision blurred so severely she could not even see the buttons properly.

"Help," she tried calling again, but the chemicals had robbed her of her voice and her plea came out as a raspy whisper. Rummaging under the small sink, she found nothing that would help her pry open the door. When her fingers skimmed a large plastic bag, neatly folded, she grabbed it and shook it open. Breath held, she fastened the bag over the trash can, hoping it would contain the fumes and buy her a few more minutes of life.

Coughing uncontrollably now, she could hardly get in a breath as she scooted to the far corner and wet a paper towel to hold over her mouth and nose. Tracy knew if she didn't get out of there in a matter of moments, she would not survive. There was no other exit from the lavatory, and though she pounded on the door, her blows were weak as the noxious gas robbed her of strength. Frantically scanning the room, she saw only one way to save her life: a small window set high up over the sink.

On shaking legs, she climbed up onto the edge, slipping

and banging her shin twice before she was able to balance on the porcelain rim. The window was old-fashioned, like the café itself, the old iron latch rusty as she tugged on it. Dizziness almost overcame her, but she held her breath and persisted until the latch yielded and she slid the window open a few precious inches. But it was not enough. She couldn't squeeze out and she lacked the strength to wrestle the window any farther.

Try to attract attention from someone outside. She grabbed an extra roll of paper towel from a shelf over the sink and held on to one edge, tossing the other end out the open window. It unrolled, a ridiculous signal, but all she could think to do. It might be enough to be noticed by a passerby, someone parking in the back lot maybe or filling the garbage dumpster.

Seconds ticked into minutes. Despair chewed at her as she thrust her head as close as she could to the window, breathing in as much fresh air as possible.

"Help," she called out in a gasping croak.

Had she heard an answer? Or was it the roaring in her own ears as her vision began to slip away? Knees shaking, she clung to the window frame.

Was that the sound of shouts at the door?

Yes, she decided as her knees crumpled and she tumbled off the sink onto the floor. Someone knew she was trapped. Keegan would come; he had to.

But the door remained shut fast as she slipped into unconsciousness.

ELEVEN

Keegan wrestled his way by several stable hands intent on clearing the building.

"Don't go back in there, buddy," one said, stiff-arming him. "Fire alarm. Can't you hear it? Something wrong with your ears?"

Keegan shoved him aside and made it back into the coffee shop. Inside, the owner was directing people out the exits. "Probably nothing," he called. "We should be back in action in a few minutes. The cook charred the bacon last week and the same thing happened."

"But what's that smell?" Meg, the waitress, asked, helping an older couple out of their booth. "It's like cleaner or something."

No, not cleaner, Keegan thought, the bottom dropping out of his stomach. He raced past the owner without explanation and down the hallway, past the kitchen, where the cook was peeling off his greasy apron and shutting down the grill.

"Dumb fire alarm again. This time it wasn't my fault!" he hollered to no one in particular. "I ain't burned nothing."

"Get out. Fumes," Keegan told the man before he ducked out again and pressed on along the hallway. The air was toxic with fumes that scalded his eyes and throat, so he grabbed a dish towel from a pile stacked on a shelf and held it over his mouth. It took another few seconds to determine that the ladies' room was the source. He pushed at the door, finding it wedged shut. Discarding the towel, he began kicking at it down low with his heel, aiming to dislodge the wedge. It remained stuck.

Sweat broke out on his forehead. Was he already too late?

Hold on, Tracy.

His eyes burned, but he kept on kicking until someone gripped his shoulder. Jack stood there with another person, the balding older guy with the denim shirt who thrust an ax into his hands.

Keegan didn't stop for introductions but began to heave the ax at the door, sending pieces flying. He aimed for the lower edge, chipping away shards of wood, chopping a hole near the wedge so he could pop it loose.

"I hear the fire department," Jack called. "I'll go send them around the back."

The stranger did not leave, brushing away the pile of debris so Keegan could have a clear shot with the ax. Another piece came loose, just above the wedge.

"Hurry," the man urged.

Keegan hefted the ax for all he was worth. Like splitting the dense oak logs on the ranch, he tried to tell himself, *Steady and even strokes*, but his fear was so thick it was choking him along with the fumes.

She'd been in there for how long? Five minutes? Ten? Long enough for the fumes to have suffocated her. Jack's soon-to-be wife would know the exact effects of the toxicity on Tracy's body. Was he going to be too late?

His ax ate away at the bottom of the door until the wedge popped loose. He handed the ax to the man, shoved the ruined door aside and charged through into a wall of choking fumes. Tracy lay on her side, eyes closed, blood trickling from her lips. He could not see if she was breathing.

Get her out of here. Now. Heart jackhammering against his ribs, he scooped her up and carried her out of the ladies' room and toward the direction of the rear exit. After only a few paces, he staggered to a stop. His eyes were streaming so badly he could not see well enough to navigate their escape.

Keep going, keep moving, he told himself, but he had become disoriented. Was he moving toward the exit or back in the direction of the deadly toxins?

The older man gripped his shoulder from behind and pressed him onward.

"This way. Fast."

After a few seconds of nerve-pounding confusion, Keegan carried Tracy outside, bursting into the blessedly clean air. He moved far enough away from the building to be free of the gas. The medics were just dismounting their rig and they hastened over, easing Tracy onto a stretcher and beginning their examination.

Owen and Barrett jogged up, taking it all in.

Jack didn't speak, just put his hand on Keegan's shoulder. Owen and Barrett touched the other, and he knew they were saying a silent prayer. He was grateful, as he could not seem to summon a single word to edge past the terror.

The medics checked for a pulse and then, with a stethoscope, her breathing. Keegan thought his heart had stopped completely until one medic called out, "Got a pulse. Breathing is shallow but she's holding her own. Pupils reactive."

Keegan's knees went weak and he wanted to press closer, to take hold of her fingers splayed out so delicate and small against the material of her jacket. If he hadn't gone outside… if he'd stayed close like he should have…

They placed an oxygen mask over her mouth while continuing to monitor her vitals.

"Does she take any medications that you know of?" asked one of the medics.

Keegan was surprised when the stranger answered.

"She used to be on anticonvulsants, but she hasn't taken them in six months."

Keegan turned to the man, head spinning. "You must be Tracy's grandfather." He offered a palm.

The man did not extend his in return. His mouth was a hard line above the stubbled chin. "I am. Name's Stew Wilson. And you must be the guy she told me about in her last phone call, Keegan something or other."

Keegan did not understand the hostility. "Keegan Thorn. I helped her out of a jam."

"Yeah? From what I'm hearing, she doesn't need your kind of help."

Keegan shot him a puzzled look.

"You're some sort of tough guy, aren't you? Ducking punches from gangsters, got a beef with Bryce Larraby and his son, the police chief, too? Yeah, I got an earful from the locals. And now this." Stew turned tortured eyes on the still figure of his granddaughter. "How much of this is because of you, I wonder?"

"Me? I'm not…"

Jack stepped between them as Owen kept his grip on Keegan's shoulder. "Not the time. Let's get her medical attention, and then we'll sort all this out."

Stew started to reply when the medics lifted Tracy into the back of the ambulance.

"I can drive you…" Keegan started.

"I'll get there by myself." Stew stalked away toward a beat-up Chevy truck.

Keegan did not know how to sort through the emotions that tumbled through him—fear for Tracy, anger, outrage.

Jack stood nearby as Keegan breathed hard.

Barrett blew out a breath. "Let him calm down. He's out of his mind with fear."

"How about you?" a medic asked Keegan. "Need medical attention?"

"No," Keegan said. His stinging eyes drifted back to the paper towels hanging limply out the window where she must have tried to signal for help, his help. All he needed was to be sure Tracy would be okay.

And to find out who exactly needed to be punished for hurting her.

Tracy woke in the ambulance and tried to protest that she didn't need a hospital, but she found herself there anyway, poked, prodded and given intravenous fluids and ointment for her burning eyes, along with something vile tasting to soothe her ravaged throat.

At the hospital, John was waiting when the doctor finished her initial treatment, and she would have groaned aloud if her grandfather hadn't stepped in front of him.

"Grandpa." Tears rolled down her face as he pressed his wide cheek to hers, the white stubble tickling her chin.

"You need a shave," she said, voice breaking.

"Hey, Honeybunch. Don't I always? You doing okay?"

The tenderness from this gruff bear of a man almost made her break down. She gulped in a steadying breath before she attempted to talk. "Someone tried to kill me. Again."

Now her grandfather shot a scathing look at John. "And what are you doing to protect my granddaughter? Some town you got here—killers run loose as they please."

The chief was respectful, but his mouth tightened as he explained, "We're looking for witnesses at the coffee shop."

"Keep looking," Keegan said as he strolled in. "Must be

one of the people who work for the horse center." He turned a gaze on her that made her heart quiver. "Hey, Pockets."

She struggled to sit straighter, nerves thrumming. "They said you pulled me out."

"Not just me, your grandpa here—"

Her grandfather cut him off. "You're not invited in this room. Family only."

"Grandpa, he's a friend."

"No, he's not, and if I hadn't rustled up the ax, you might not be alive to talk about it."

Tracy let out a breath. She didn't know why her grandfather was being so unfriendly to Keegan Thorn, but she was used to his irascible nature and overprotectiveness. "I'm glad you both worked together."

Her grandfather's eyes went steely. "Well, that won't be happening again. From now on, I'm taking care of you up at the property. He's not needed."

She looked from Keegan, who was stony-faced, to John, who revealed the tiniest expression of satisfaction that his half brother was the subject of her grandfather's ire.

"What happened today wasn't Keegan's fault. Someone wants to kill me—the same person who murdered a woman at the horse center. I believe the victim was a veterinarian who worked there, Nan Ridley."

"That shouldn't be too hard to prove, if she's been killed." Grandpa Stew folded his arms and waited for the chief to reply.

John seemed to be considering how much to share. "We've left messages for Ms. Ridley at her vet office and with her neighbors. No one knows where she's gone, but that isn't unexpected, as she was a very private person. Her office is closed for a month while workers re-carpet and paint. Ostensibly, she timed that work to coincide with her stint at the horse center."

Tracy slapped a hand on the edge of the bed in frustration. "She must have told someone where she was going. Family?"

John shrugged. "There's an ex-husband in Fresno we're trying to locate, but it's doubtful whether she'd have filled him in on this last-minute job in Phoenix. She's not active on social media except for a Facebook page for her vet office. Dad—I mean, Bryce Larraby—confirmed she gave her notice and quit unexpectedly, which is why he hired a replacement."

"We'll keep looking," Keegan said. "Digging. My family and I…"

"No," John said. "You'll stay out of it."

"I don't answer to you," Keegan said.

"Well, maybe you'll answer to me, then," Stew Wilson said, puffing up his chest.

"Grandpa…"

He waved her off. "I don't care about what happened at the center, or this Nan person, or the beef between you two, or your father's involvement. The police can clean up this mess. All I care about is my granddaughter's safety, and I will see to that myself."

"Grandpa," Tracy said again, but a coughing fit stopped her words. All three men looked at her with concern.

A nurse entered with a paper cup full of pills. She clucked disapprovingly. "You need to rest, Ms. Wilson. The doctor told you that extreme stress and fatigue can be precursors to another seizure."

"I heard what he said." Tracy was mortified that the nurse had been so indiscreet with her private health information. It was bad enough that John already figured she was a head case.

Her grandfather stepped closer. "Is it likely? Should she stay here?"

"I am not staying here," Tracy said, "and I am not going to have another seizure. I'm done with that medicine protocol."

Her grandfather did not look convinced, but the nurse seemed to remember her professionalism. "Excuse me, gentlemen. The doctor wants to examine Ms. Wilson one more time before we talk about discharging her, so you'll need to wait outside."

"I will wait," her grandfather said. "I'm family."

"I'll wait, too." Keegan's eyes flashed and she saw the reddening flush in her grandfather's cheeks.

"Don't stick around where you're not wanted," John said.

Not wanted. She saw Keegan flinch and knew in that moment it was the core of his anger, the fuel for his rage. It was not solely that Bryce Larraby had mistreated his mother; it sprang from the deepest hurt of all—the pain of being an unwanted child.

"Keegan," she said, palm outstretched to him. *I want you.* Her thoughts left her dumbstruck. It could not be in her to want this wild and wounded man. Her cheeks burned as if she had said it aloud.

But he was already gone, the door swinging shut behind him.

TWELVE

For the first time in his life, Keegan was not hungry. He played with the pot roast and declined a biscuit. His mother, father, Owen and Barrett exchanged shocked looks. Jack no doubt would have, as well, but he'd flown his Cessna to pick up Shannon for a quick visit home for dress fittings and a bridal shower before the end of her last week of residency and the wedding.

Keegan could not get Stew's remarks out of his mind. If he hadn't been tussling with Sonny, if his relationship with his father and half brother wasn't quite so contentious…

"Look, I'll just be the one to state the obvious," Owen said, "but none of this is your fault."

"I don't want to talk about it," Keegan said. He was not sure what would come out of his mouth. All he could feel was the heavy thumping of his heart, along with a hefty dose of worry for Tracy. Worry was not something he was accustomed to, and now he could not seem to shake the feeling.

"All right," his mother said. She got up and brought a box of materials to the table. "Then you can help me fold the wedding place cards. Shelby has volunteered to fill them out, but I'm not sure that baby is going to wait too much longer."

Barrett went pale and gulped audibly.

"Steady." Owen gave him a whack on the back. "We've delivered plenty of foals over the years. Birth is a natural process."

"I'd like to see you try it," his mother said, which sent them all into chuckles.

Keegan allowed a smile but it didn't last long. He folded the place cards mechanically while his mind traveled along the only helpful path he could think of, the trail that might lead him to the truth about Nan Ridley. He'd spent a restless hour poring over any mention of her on the web and his half brother was right: she was a very private person.

"Did you find any social-media activity for Nan?" he asked Ella, who had joined him at the table after wheeling her sister, Betsy, into position first. Ella was far more savvy with Facebook and the like than he'd ever be.

He smiled at Betsy and handed her some cards to fold. She gave him a small smile in return, eager to help as always, even if she could not communicate her feelings in words.

"Nothing. Only a business Facebook page. Her profile is professional, nothing of a personal nature to indicate any friends or hobbies."

Hobbies. The word made him sit straight as he recalled a tiny detail he'd stumbled across earlier. "Wait a minute. The minis."

His mother arched an eyebrow. "Cars or horses?"

"Horses. Somewhere in one of the searches, it said she'd raised miniature horses as a kid. She provided pro bono care to rescued minis, so she probably donated some time at that outfit in Star Valley."

Ella snapped her fingers. "Little Hooves Ranch. I know the place. You can go talk to the owner." She squinted.

"Her name is Lorna. I made some custom horseshoes for her several years ago."

Keegan leaped up from the table. "Great idea."

"Well, you can't go now," his mother said. "It's almost seven at night, and it's freezing."

"I'm driving up to Tracy's property to tell her. Bring her some wood, too, for the fireplace."

"You could call her," Ella suggested with a calculating look.

He grabbed a cookie from the plate on the counter. Now he had a plan, something to do to help her, to make up for the problems he'd caused her. His appetite returned in full force. "Cell phone coverage is spotty there, and besides, I want to take up a generator since they don't have electricity."

Evie got up immediately. After pulling plastic containers from the cupboards, she began loading up leftover pot roast and biscuits along with a dozen gingerbread cookies and bean salad. "For Tracy and her grandfather," she said sternly. "I don't want you to eat all the cookies on your way up."

He laughed and kissed his mother. "You figure a food peace offering will make Grandpa Stew like me better?"

He had not gotten the chuckle he'd intended. Instead she put a warm and calloused hand to his cheek. "Just show him who you are, Keegan, the tender man you keep in here." She put a finger to his chest.

He caught her hand and pressed a kiss to her knuckles. "I never deserved a home like this," he whispered.

"Yes, you did, honey. Everyone deserves a home like this."

Heart brimming with love he could not express, arms burdened with his mother's offerings, he hurried out the door into the freezing night.

* * *

Tracy shivered as her grandfather blew patiently on the wood. "Too wet," he grumbled. "No one thought to cover the woodpile."

She wished she had another cough drop to soothe the burning in her throat. "No one has lived here for a decade," she reminded him. "That's why we got it for a song."

"More like a full-on opera. Wiped out both our savings pretty good." He got to his feet.

"We're gonna make it," Tracy said. "And Dad would be proud." She mumbled, "Maybe Mom will be, too, someday."

"Your mother is too stiff-necked to ever let go of what Matt did. Wrong of her to punish you for loving your dad."

It was a conversation they'd had many times before. Right or wrong, she still yearned for a relationship with her mother and a piece inside her would always remain hollow and empty without that reconciliation.

"Can't figure out why you aren't plenty angry about it," he continued.

"I was, for a long time, but Dad forgave her even though she couldn't forgive him. I guess…" She shrugged. "Dad said forgiveness isn't a two-way street." Her throat closed up and she found she could not go on, so deep was her longing for her father.

Grandpa Stew wrapped her in an embrace. "I miss him, too, Honeybunch."

When she had no more tears to cry, she checked the doors of the drafty three-bedroom cabin. They were locked with heavy brass bolts. The windows did not have fasteners, but she'd found the casing so rusted shut they might as well have locks. The kitchen was still a mess, with boxes piled onto the old tile counter, but at least two beds were made up with secondhand sheets she'd purchased on her previous visit.

How could her life have been turned upside down in only a matter of days? The last time she'd been here, she'd been thrilled to feather the cozy nest, to start investigating the area for possible connections that would help her career and their dream of opening a lodge. The Silver Spurs horse show had seemed like a dream come true, and the Mother Lode was one of the reasons she'd considered the area in the first place.

Such an auspicious beginning, and what a snare she was now firmly entangled in.

She walked to the window and looked out into the night. The wrinkled foothills were just visible in the moonlight against a clear, starry sky. Several old cabins stood silhouetted in the chill. Most were uninhabitable and would need to be razed and rebuilt, along with a bigger stable and corrals.

Her feet felt like ice, proving the weathermen right when they'd predicted a freeze. They might even get a dusting of snow. Keegan had a point that occupying the cabin without electricity was probably foolish.

Her heart squeezed as she recalled the look on Keegan's face when John put him in his place.

You're not wanted here.

And her own strange response.

I want you.

At that moment she ached for his smile, one of his cocky jokes, the earnestness of his nosy questions.

Stop it, Tracy.

He was not part of the plan and she'd learned long ago that it was costly to invest in others.

Take care of Grandpa and keep to yourself.

Perhaps once the investigation was resolved she could resurrect that anonymity she craved, the quiet life that was the key to her happiness.

Pulling the curtains closed, she went to seek the solace of her bed. It was only eight thirty, but she felt like her legs would not hold her up any longer. "I'll just lie down for an hour and then I'll unpack more boxes," she told her grandfather.

Grandpa was content to read an old copy of the *Farmer's Almanac* by the light of one of the lanterns she'd purchased. She'd never admit it to him, but it made her feel safer knowing that her grandfather would be on watch for a while, even though the property was far away from the horse center and the town of Gold Bar, where she'd almost lost her life a second time.

She'd closed her eyes for what seemed only a moment, but something jolted her awake. Her phone told her it was almost ten o'clock. The cabin was quiet, cold as a grave.

She heard the creak of old floorboards and fear iced over her ability to move. Someone was in the cabin. Her earlier terror returned. Throat and eyes burning, she imagined she was suffocating again, crumpling under an onslaught of poison.

Her brain supplied some measure of calm to her thundering nerves. The noise was her grandfather, of course. In spite of the winter-weight blankets, she was shivering. He must be cold, as well. Maybe he was trying to start the fire again. She let out a breath and pulled boots over her two pairs of socks. Might as well get some boxes unpacked since she was awake.

She reached for the battery-powered lantern and switched it on. Easing down the hallway, she emerged in the living room. The fireplace was dark—no sign of her grandfather.

Maybe he had gone to his room. She headed back the way she had come when a hand clamped on her arm.

She screamed.

"Hush," her grandfather whispered. "Someone's out there."

Her body went rigid. Vision adjusting slowly to the darkness, she sucked in a breath when she realized he was holding a shotgun with one hand.

"Grandpa..." she started.

"I heard a motorcycle. Saw a headlamp coming up the mountain. Then it switched off. Someone doesn't want us to know they're here."

"I'll try to call the police. I almost got a signal from the back bedroom." Pulse pounding, she scurried down the hallway. In the farthest room, which was piled with boxes yet to be unloaded, she attempted to dial 9-1-1, but though she tried every corner of the room, she got no signal. Skin prickled with fear, she hurried back.

A blast of icy air robbed her of breath. *No!* her mind screamed as her eyes interpreted the scene.

The living room was empty. Her grandfather was gone and the front door was banging in the winter breeze.

THIRTEEN

Keegan heard the blast of a shotgun. Forgetting the care packages he'd been about to retrieve, he took off sprinting for the dark cabin.

Why didn't I bring my rifle? he chastised himself. As he charged up the weed-covered walkway, he wondered if he was heading right into the line of fire. Was Tracy shooting? His chest tightened. Or was someone shooting at her?

He was almost to the door when Tracy came out with such speed that she plowed right into him.

He grabbed her shoulders. "What's wrong?"

"Keegan?" Gulping in air, she squeezed her arms around his torso. He could feel her heart ramming into her ribs, muscles quivering. As she pulled away, the moonlight reflected her stark terror back at him. "What...what are you doing here?" she gasped.

"Later. Who's shooting?"

"I think it's Grandpa. He heard someone out there, a motorcycle, and he went after them."

"Which direction?"

"I don't know."

He turned her around. "Go back in the house. Lock the doors. I'll find him."

"FAST FIVE" READER SURVEY

Your participation entitles you to:
✳ **4 Thank-You Gifts Worth Over $20!**

Complete the survey in minutes.

Get **2 FREE Books**

See inside for details.

Dear Reader,

Since you are a lover of our books, your opinions are important to us... and so is your time.

That's why we made sure your **"FAST FIVE" READER SURVEY** can be completed in just a few minutes. Your answers to the five questions will help us remain at the forefront of women's fiction.

And, as a thank-you for participating, we'd like to send you **4 FREE THANK-YOU GIFTS!**

Enjoy your gifts with our appreciation,

Pam Powers

To get your
4 FREE THANK-YOU GIFTS:

✷ Quickly complete the "Fast Five" Reader Survey
and return the insert.

"FAST FIVE" READER SURVEY

1	Do you sometimes read a book a second or third time?	○ Yes	○ No
2	Do you often choose reading over other forms of entertainment such as television?	○ Yes	○ No
3	When you were a child, did someone regularly read aloud to you?	○ Yes	○ No
4	Do you sometimes take a book with you when you travel outside the home?	○ Yes	○ No
5	In addition to books, do you regularly read newspapers and magazines?	○ Yes	○ No

YES! I have completed the above Reader Survey. Please send me my 4 FREE GIFTS (gifts worth over $20 retail). I understand that I am under no obligation to buy anything, as explained on the back of this card.

❏ I prefer the regular-print edition
153/353 IDL GM3W

❏ I prefer the larger-print edition
107/307 IDL GM3W

FIRST NAME   LAST NAME

ADDRESS

APT.#   CITY

STATE/PROV.   ZIP/POSTAL CODE

Offer limited to one per household and not applicable to series that subscriber is currently receiving.
Your Privacy—The Reader Service is committed to protecting your privacy. Our Privacy Policy is available online at www.ReaderService.com or upon request from the Reader Service. We make a portion of our mailing list available to reputable third parties that offer products we believe may interest you. If you prefer that we not exchange your name with third parties, or if you wish to clarify or modify your communication preferences, please visit us at www.ReaderService.com/consumerchoice or write to us at Reader Service Preference Service, P.O. Box 9062, Buffalo, NY 14240-9062. Include your complete name and address.   SLI-817-FF18

"Not without me, you won't. He could be hurt, and besides, he's liable to shoot at you."

"A family hobby, it seems."

"I'm going."

"Tracy…"

"There," she said, stabbing a finger at one of the dilapidated cabins. "I saw something moving. It has to be Grandpa."

"Or the intruder," he snapped. She started off but he grabbed her wrist. "If you're gonna be all bullheaded, Pockets, at least stay behind me." He shoved her around his back and scrambled toward the cabin, keeping to the fringe of trees.

They approached quickly, the soft ground muffling their steps. About twenty feet from the cabin they crouched behind a fallen pine, listening. An owl hooted softly in the distance and wind ruffled the tall grasses. He thought he heard the distant rumble of a vehicle speeding down the mountain, but he could not be sure.

"Can you text him?" Keegan whispered.

"He doesn't have a cell phone."

"Of course he doesn't." Keegan sighed. "I guess we'll have to do this the hard way. Stay here."

"I…"

Before she could raise a ruckus, he crept out from their hiding place and put some distance between him and Tracy. "Mr. Wilson?" he called out. "It's Keegan Thorn."

He heard a groan.

Tracy whimpered.

"Are you injured?" Keegan called.

Stew's voice, rough and gravelly, came from the bleak interior. "I told you to stay off this property, and I meant it."

Keegan squared his shoulders. "Well, I'm here anyway,

and I know I've got a lot of bad qualities, but how about not shooting me, huh? That will make a big mess for you to clean up. I'm pretty sure I got a lot of blood in me."

"Grandpa," Tracy called out. "I'm with Keegan. We're coming in to help you right now. Don't you do any more shooting, you hear me?"

Keegan didn't wait for Tracy to pass him but pushed his way into the rotting cabin, skin crawling at the thought of a bullet plowing into his sternum at any moment. Better him than Tracy, though. If she would just stay out while he sized up the situation.

The planked floor was spongy under his boots, the ceiling above sagging under the accumulation of pine needles, necessitating that he slouch. The place reeked of mold, and moss grew across the wood walls. At first he thought he'd been mistaken—the place looked empty—until he saw Stew sitting on the floor. His leg was twisted awkwardly, gun in his hand.

Tracy gasped and ran to him. "What happened? Are you hurt?"

"Saw the bike coming over the top of the hill. It was you, wasn't it?" He glared at Keegan. "Got off a couple of warning shots from in here, just to send you a message. Would have shot out your tires if I hadn't sunk into the floor at this rotten patch."

"You weren't shooting at me," Keegan said. "But we've got other issues. Let's see how bad you're hurt."

His mouth pinched in pain and anger. "You stay away from me and my granddaughter. If I hadn't fallen, I would have plugged you proper and you'd have deserved it."

"Don't say that," Tracy breathed.

And they say I'm a hothead. Keegan simply knelt and ripped up the rotted board to expose the man's ankle. He shone his phone flashlight into the hole. "Hard to tell in this light. Might be broken, but you can't walk on it, that's certain. I'll carry you back to the cabin."

He made to haul Stew from his sitting position, but the man waved the shotgun in his face. "You will not."

"Grandpa!" Tracy cried out.

"Didn't you hear what I said, boy?" His eyes gleamed in the pungent darkness. "I shot at you and I meant it. Don't make me do it again, 'cause this time I'm not gonna miss."

"Shoot me if you have to," Keegan said, "but one thing you should know first. The intruder you fired at wasn't me."

"Likely story," Stew snapped.

Keegan bit down the rising irritation. "You said you shot at a motorcycle."

"Yeah."

"You sure about that?"

"I know my engines. It was a motorcycle."

He stared right back at Tracy's grandfather as he delivered the news. "I drove a truck, Mr. Wilson. My bike is back at the ranch."

Silence. The words drifted, held for a moment in the dank space. Stew's mouth fell open and Keegan took the opportunity to haul him off the floor and get a shoulder under one of his armpits. Tracy helped support him from the other side and they began to carry him back to the cabin. On the way, Keegan tried to listen for the sound of a motor, but he heard nothing over the wind and Grandpa Stew's groaning protests. The man was still trying to digest Keegan's revelation.

At any other moment Keegan would have enjoyed besting Tracy's cantankerous relative, but the truth bunched up the muscles in his gut.

No one would be riding their motorcycle onto the property at this hour by accident.

The motorcyclist had come on purpose. To find Tracy. His fear supplied the rest.
And kill her.

Tracy did not allow herself to feel, just to do. *Take care of Grandpa. That's all.*

Feet numb from the cold, they hauled her grandfather to the cabin and set him on the sofa. After piling fleece blankets on top of him, she turned on the lanterns and examined his ankle.

"Lock the door behind me," Keegan said. While she watched from behind the curtain, he ran to his truck and brought in an armful of dry wood.

Soon he was busy coaxing a fire to life. The crackling flames sounded sweeter than music to her ears, the tang of smoke more tantalizing than a delicious meal. The fire would chase away the terror and the shadows.

Don't be such a child, she chided, but relief swelled above the trepidation as the wood caught. She was so terribly grateful that Keegan had arrived when he had. A lock of dark hair fell across his forehead as he stoked the fire, broad shoulders encased in a scarred leather jacket. From head to the worn soles of his boots, Keegan was a cowboy, mixed with something much more dangerous. Her grandfather was right; he was a rebel, a trouble magnet, but at that moment she nearly wept with relief to have him there.

Fighting for control, she pulled the curtains tightly closed and activated a chemical ice pack from the first-aid kit she'd brought. The warmth of the fire and Keegan's steadying presence allowed her to focus on the thought she'd kept at bay. Someone had tracked her to the property. Panic bubbled up her throat again, but she shoved it down.

She gently prodded her grandfather's ankle, earning a

groan that he could not contain. "I'm not sure if it's broken or not. You'll need an X-ray."

Keegan sat back on his knees, feeding kindling slowly into the flames. "We'll get him to a hospital as soon as we're positive the biker's gone and I can get one of my brothers here to keep watch. Already called the police from my truck after I did another check."

"How did you…?"

"I brought a satellite phone for you to keep here. Mama insists we have one since we have this penchant for going camping out in the boonies. The cops are sending a unit."

"So we can look forward to more drama between you and John Larraby?" her grandfather snarled.

Keegan kept his attention on the flames. "You're on unincorporated land. Gold Bar is the nearest police department. John's the one in charge."

"And that means we have to rely on your brother, the one who can't stand you?"

A muscle in his jaw jumped. "Half brother, and the feeling is mutual, but he'll do his job like he would for any other citizen."

It was the nearest thing to a compliment she'd ever heard Keegan say about John. She hoped he really believed it deep down.

Her grandfather shook his head. "Anyway, I'm not going to a hospital for a little wrenched ankle." In spite of his flippant tone, there was a sheen of sweat on his brow. "Been through plenty worse than this. Tore up my knee from a spooked horse one time."

Keegan chuckled. "Been there myself. Got my nose broken by a spirited mare. Took me a long time to get her to like me."

Grandpa Stew's eyes narrowed. "Ever wrangle sheep?"

"Cattle," Keegan said. "I train cutting horses."

Tracy watched her grandpa file that away in his mind. He distrusted anyone who wasn't a horse man, but didn't want to acknowledge that Keegan might have some admirable attributes. It almost made her smile.

Keegan tapped out a message on his phone. "My brothers are already on their way. Owen and Barrett are going to take the back roads. They'll make sure whoever it was isn't hanging out in the woods or something. They'll check places the cops can't."

Hanging out in the woods. A shiver rippled up her spine. *Who might be out there...waiting for Keegan to leave?* She swallowed. "Why...why did you come?"

"To give you the phone and some dry wood, and to tell you something I learned." Keegan relayed the mini-horse connection, and she felt her pulse thump harder.

"You think Nan might have said something there about her plans?" Something that would either confirm Tracy's version of the events or disprove them?

"Only one way to find out." He looked at his phone again. "Brothers are en route and cops are going to drive the main road. Whoever it was has probably split by now." He glanced at her grandfather and blew out a breath. "Shall we begin Operation Hospital Transport when my brothers arrive?"

"I told you, I'm not going."

Keegan chuckled. "Okay, then we'll go with plan B." He tapped another message into his phone, got up, grabbed the shotgun and headed for the door.

"That's my gun. Where do you think you're going?" her grandfather demanded.

"To my truck."

"Why?"

"Because if you're not going to the hospital, we're gonna bring a doctor to you, and since that's gonna take a while, I figured it's a good time for a late dinner. I'm starved."

Tracy blinked. "You're going to get dinner? Right now?"

His grin teased her nerves into a flutter. "It's in my truck, along with a generator, because there's no reason to eat a fine meal like Mama's pot roast sitting in the dark. You eat with your eyes first, you know. Mama packed some bean salad and bread for the vegetarian types." He pulled back the edge of the curtain and peered out. "I'm certain the bad guy's gone, but just in case, lock the door behind me again." He wiggled his eyebrows in comic fashion. "When I come back, I'll knock and give you the secret password."

She giggled. "What exactly is that?"

"We'll think of something, Pockets," he said, giving her an elaborate wink and handing her the shotgun.

She watched him go and dutifully locked the door behind him. Turning, she found her grandfather staring at her.

"He's trouble, and you've had enough of that to last a lifetime."

She fussed with the blanket she'd placed over him. "He's just a friend."

"A friend who's using you to get back at his kin. Or maybe for the excitement. He's an adrenaline junkie, I'm guessing. I've met plenty of those kinds of guys. Never any good."

"Like I said, he's just a friend."

His tone grew gentler. "Tracy, you don't need friends like that, the kind who are gonna disappoint you and let you down."

And how profoundly her friends had, when it became public knowledge in their small town that her father had gone to jail for assault. Her mother had practically turned into a recluse at that point, shielding Tracy's five-year-old sister, Lily, as best she could.

Tracy was another matter. At age seventeen she'd had to face the judgment of her high school peers, and she'd thought she'd die of mortification. Then when he'd been released and she'd made the choice to go live with him as a high school senior, people she'd thought were her friends— the few she'd managed to hold on to—disappeared. It was as if her father had a contagious disease and no one wanted to risk contamination from being near his daughter. That was when she'd learned to be alone, quiet, invisible.

Grandpa sought her hand and pressed her fingers to his rough cheek. "I don't want to see you get hurt anymore, Tracy, and Keegan Thorn has heartbreak written all over him. Trust your old grandpa on this, Honeybunch."

She kissed him. "I do, Grandpa."

"Then send him on his way after dinner. I can protect us, and we've got the cops involved now."

"He just wants to help me."

"No, he wants to help himself. Send him away, Tracy."

"I will," she found herself saying, but she wondered why she felt a pain deep inside when she did.

Keegan Thorn has heartbreak written all over him.

And Tracy did not intend to let him have the chance to prove her grandfather right, no matter what her heart said about it.

FOURTEEN

Shannon and Jack arrived just after midnight, right after Barrett and Owen finished their check and reported in. Keegan thought Shannon looked tired from her emergency room duties, but she was as efficient as ever, hugging Keegan and shaking Tracy's hand. She cheerfully but assertively pushed Stew's objections aside and examined his ankle in spite of his protests.

"I'm going to surmise it's not broken, but that's just a shot in the dark. An X-ray would be the most prudent course of action, but I'm used to stubborn cowboy types refusing proper medical attention." That earned her a smile from both Stew and Jack.

Stew straightened on the sofa and puffed up a bit. "Messed myself up a lot worse wrangling sheep in my time."

"I'm sure you have. Stay off of it and do an ice regimen for the next few days." She offered him a pair of crutches and handed Tracy a supply of reusable ice packs.

Shannon stifled a yawn.

Tracy grasped her arm. "Thank you, for coming all this way. I know you must be exhausted with your residency and the wedding plans and such."

Shannon flipped back her curtain of dark hair. "Oh, I

can never get enough time with Jack, so I was happy to drive up here to your place." She paused and spoke softly. "I understand you had a head injury among other things. Any headaches? Blurred vision?"

"Just some mild headaches. Nothing serious."

"Memories coming back?"

"Snippets is all, in no particular order." Tracy huffed out a breath. "So frustrating."

"Brains heal slowly." Shannon patted her arm. "All you can do is be patient."

Not easy when the bad guys are circling like wolves, Keegan thought.

She looked at Keegan. "How about you, tough guy? Shoulder healing okay?"

Keegan flexed like a bodybuilder. "You may call me the Iron Cowboy."

They all laughed, Shannon loudest of all. "Right. I'll try to remember that."

Jack looped an arm around her. "Gotta get this doc home for some sleep. She's got a dress fitting and then it's back to the hospital until just before the wedding." He kissed the side of her cheek and suddenly the in-charge doctor was a giggling little girl again, pressing her cheek to Jack's.

Keegan's eyes drifted to Tracy and he thought again that she was possibly the most beautiful woman he'd ever met. Physically pretty, yes, but something about her calm spirit, her ability to be both quiet and courageous at the same time, also drew him to her. He wanted her close, not for the fun and adventures he usually enjoyed with other women, but because of the way his spirit eased when she was next to him. She brought him joy, but joy did not last as long as the pain of betrayal. Keegan knew he wasn't cut from good partner material, and he didn't want to break Tracy's heart.

But still the longing remained inside him, reverberating low and sonorous like rolling thunder.

He realized he was staring, shook away the cloudy thoughts and walked Shannon and Jack to the door.

"Ready for Cyclone?" Jack asked.

Keegan nodded. Jack opened the door and whistled. In a moment, a black-and-white border collie bounded in, tail wagging. He immediately sniffed everything he could get to before stopping to greet each person.

"Who's this?" Tracy said, bending to fondle his ears.

"Cyclone's the best herding dog in the county," Keegan said. He noticed Grandpa Stew leaned over to get a look. "He's also got ears like a bat. Great protection dog."

"Don't need any dog," Grandpa Stew said, but there wasn't much fire behind the words as the dog went over to give him a sniff. Keegan thought he detected a quirk on Grandpa Stew's mouth that might have passed for the seed of a smile.

"Just for a few days, maybe," Tracy said.

Keegan shrugged casually. "Sure. Until things settle down. Jack brought plenty of food for him, and he'll be sniffing every square inch of your property come dawn. Dog's built for adventure."

Shannon stifled another yawn and Jack led her toward the door.

"Coming home soon?" Jack asked.

"I'm bunking here," Keegan announced. As he'd expected, Grandpa Stew bristled, but Keegan held up a hand. "I'm fine on the couch, or I can sleep in the truck, but I'm not leaving you two alone up here tonight, not until I get a look at the locks in the daylight and I'm sure you're secure."

Grandpa Stew grumbled until Tracy knelt next to him. "He's right, Grandpa."

The man continued to voice his discontent, but his volume diminished until he grabbed the crutches and, with Tracy's help, hobbled to his room. Cyclone trotted after him, and the old man did not shoo him away. Keegan had gotten the generator up and running, so the cabin was now lit, and the two continued their cautious way along.

"If you need anything—" Jack started.

"We won't." Keegan urged them to the door. "Go take your fiancée home before Mama comes looking for you both."

"Good night, Keegan," Shannon said. "I mean, Iron Cowboy."

With a sigh, Jack followed her out, and Keegan locked the door behind them.

Tracy returned. "Cyclone decided to bunk with Grandpa. Amazing."

"He likes old rancher types. He's probably hoping there will be livestock to wrangle tomorrow. It's his life's work to wrangle cows, but if there aren't any around, he'll settle for people. I think he's decided to keep tabs on your grandpa."

Tracy frowned. "I appreciate the extra pair of eyes on him. With everything that's going on, I haven't paid enough attention to the Silver Spurs Horse Show. The opening ceremony is tomorrow, right?"

Keegan nodded, grimacing as he pictured his father beaming at the crowds, welcoming them as if he were the president, rather than the mayor of a small California town.

She continued, arms wrapped around herself. "As much as I'd rather never set foot in the Mother Lode again, I need to take another look at Flight before the auction bidding starts on Wednesday and the crowds arrive for the weekend events."

"I'll go with you, right after we visit the minis."

"Keegan…"

"Hey, we're transporting six horses down tomorrow from the Gold Bar and my cutting competition is Friday night, so we'll be all over that place anyway."

She was quiet, mulling over how to keep him away, he figured. Apparently his strange desire to have her close did not work in reverse. She preferred being alone and she'd said as much.

He yawned widely. "Time for some shut-eye." He turned to lie down on the couch.

"No need for that. You can have your own space, if you don't mind the clutter."

She showed him to a tiny room just past her own and the one Grandpa Stew occupied. The generator enabled her to turn on a ceramic lamp, which revealed boxes stacked neatly along the wall, waiting to be unpacked. There was a cot with a sleeping bag still rolled up on top.

"Not exactly fancy."

"Plenty fancy enough for me. Thanks." The lamplight wreathed her in pale ivory and caught flecks of gold in her hair, the sweet curve of her lower lip caught between her teeth.

"Um, well, shout if you need anything," she said, knocking over a small box as she turned, sending a scatter of beads across the floor. She got on all fours to retrieve them as he chased after some that rolled away.

He handed her his finds. "Making some jewelry?"

She nodded. "Bracelets for my mom and sister. Christmas presents."

"Nice."

Her eyes were wide, filled with some strong emotion.

"Talk to me, Pockets," he said softly.

"It's nothing."

"Not nothing."

"They probably won't see me so I can deliver them. My mom…well, she hasn't forgiven me for choosing to live with my dad after he got out of prison, and she's kept my sister away from me, too. I've missed so many big moments in her life. I can't believe she's in high school. Sometimes she'll text me." Her cheeks flushed. "It's dumb, but I print all the texts and glue them in a journal. I guess it's my way of pretending that we have a relationship of some sort."

"I'm sorry," he said, touching her arm.

She offered a shaky smile. "It's okay. I just keep trying. I'll always keep trying."

One tear trickled down her cheek and she caught it with the back of her hand as if embarrassed to let it fall.

He was mesmerized.

What kind of courage did that take? To forgive and even patiently pursue people who had wronged you grievously? He found it was a chore to pull in a full breath, searching for a joke, a glib remark to lighten the mood, and finding none at all. "That's… You're pretty amazing."

She blinked. "Me? No. Not me."

"Yes, you." And then somehow he'd taken her by the shoulders and pulled her into the circle of his embrace, her silky hair tickling his neck, his arms containing the softness of her slender body, feeling a rush of comfort he knew he was not entitled to.

"Thank you," she whispered against his chest. "I mean, for what you did tonight. I'm sorry my grandpa is so rough on you."

"He's right. I've been a troublemaker for most of my life. Lately, though…" His eyes found hers as he tipped her chin up. "I wonder if it isn't better to be more like you— quiet, settled." He could not help himself as he stroked a finger along her cheek. Her breath quickened but she did not move away, so he pressed a kiss to her temple, kept his lips there, feeling the softness and the strength of her. It made him long for something, something altogether different from the fun and adventure he'd sought from his past relationships. Whatever it was, the feeling hovered there, formless, nebulous, overwhelming. As he lowered his mouth to find hers, she stepped back.

"Well, um, good night." She almost sprinted from the room.

He sighed. *Smooth, Keeg. Tracy's scared to be close to you, and Grandpa Stew would like to shoot you. Seems like you've muddled things up enough for one night, huh?*

Finding the camping cot in the corner of the room, he unfurled the sleeping bag, kicked off his boots and lay down, listening to the noises of the night.

Tracy was startled the next morning to awaken to the smell of coffee. She jerked upright, and it took her a moment to put together the warm, comforting aroma with the flood of terror from the night before. Grandpa shooting… an intruder…the way her lungs still burned from the gas that had almost killed her at the café. Then she remembered that Keegan was on the premises, and her cheeks warmed thinking of the way he'd touched her, kissed her.

After a couple of fortifying breaths, she pulled on jeans, a warm T-shirt and fuzzy socks, then padded into the kitchen past her grandpa's closed door.

Keegan was staring out the kitchen window over the rim of a steaming coffee mug, the thumb of his free hand hooked in the pocket of his faded jeans. His cowboy hat lay on the table. Startled from his reverie, he smiled and poured her a cup of coffee.

"Couldn't find sugar."

"Black's fine," she said. "You didn't have to make coffee."

"I'm the first one up at the ranch every day. It's my self-appointed job, plus I can sneak a slice of bread and jam before anyone else cracks an eyeball."

She laughed. "I have bread we can toast."

He grinned like he'd just earned a rodeo ribbon. "Mama packed some of her apricot jam with the dinner provisions. She's giving away jars of it as Christmas gifts." He fell quiet as she toasted the bread. "Tracy, my brother is on his way up. Should be here any minute."

"Which brother?"

His tone was brittle. "The cop."

Nerves jangled as she handed him a slice of toast. "For what reason?"

"Wanted to tell us something, and he wouldn't cough it up over the phone. Certainly not to me, anyway. Said he couldn't get through to your phone. It's probably nothing. He just likes to be the big-deal cop and flash his badge around."

"You said last night he's a good cop."

"I guess he is, but I don't know where his loyalty lies—to his job or to his kin."

"But he's your kin, Keegan," she said quietly.

"Purely an accident of DNA."

"DNA is a pretty strong connection."

He shrugged. "We share only my father's genes, the part of me I wish I didn't have."

"Well, I'm glad you have Larraby in you."

He jerked a look at her.

"I wouldn't want you to be anything else but who you are."

He paused a beat. "My father is a deadbeat dad, a womanizer." There was poison in the words.

"And my dad was a convicted felon." Her eyes did not waver from his. "Good and bad and ugly mixed together all up inside me, but I'm more than my genes. I'm the choices I make." She cocked her head at him. "You are, too."

"I know I'm not like my dad."

"You work really hard so others know it, too, but you don't have to spend so much energy." She was talking too much, but the thoughts just flowed out as if his caress the night before had transferred some of his recklessness to her. "You're kind, loyal, funny, and you know God. That's enough."

Speechless, blue eyes wide as if she'd told him something scandalous, the glib mask he always sported dropped away. She saw the yearning there of a young boy, desperate for love, crying out for acceptance. He was the master of the joke and the smile and the caper to hide what lingered deep down below.

Slowly she put her hand over his.

He stared at the connection as if he'd never seen his own fingers before. Then his gaze traveled, blue and wondering, until it met hers.

She smiled, hoping to coax one from him.

The knock on the door made him bolt from the chair, leaving her to wonder what his response to her boldness would have been.

Probably a joke and a quick retreat. Better you hadn't said it at all.

He let John in, just as her grandfather hobbled into the kitchen on his crutches with Cyclone glued to his side.

"Dog snores," her grandfather said, easing into a chair.

"So do you," Tracy said, kissing him on the cheek. She patted the dog and offered water and kibble before letting him outside.

John was in uniform and he accepted the cup of coffee

she handed him but declined the toast. She slid a piece in front of her grandfather, too.

"I'm here because I wanted to give you a report. We did find motorcycle tire tracks in the mud at the bottom of the grade. No sign of the driver."

"I figured," Tracy said. "Thank you for looking."

"I'll have an officer cruise through whenever we can spare him."

"Thank you." She paused. "I'm thinking you have something else to tell me."

He chugged some coffee. "Fingerprints came back on the tree ornament, the new one that didn't match the others."

Tracy went still. "Whose were they?"

He cleared his throat. "Regina Parker's."

Keegan whistled. "Didn't see that coming."

"She said it's part of her office duties to keep the place neat. Says she found a box of those ornaments on the office desk Thursday afternoon and replaced the broken one, put the extras in the storage room."

Keegan frowned. "She could be lying."

"Yes," he admitted, "but there's one other thing you should know. Mitch Arnold got a text this morning."

Tracy put down her coffee. "Yes?"

"It was a text from Nan Ridley."

FIFTEEN

On the way to the Little Hooves Ranch, Tracy's mind leaped and cavorted like a new colt. She sat squashed between Keegan and her grandfather, Cyclone secured in the truck bed, wind whipping his fur and tongue flapping.

John's info scrolled through her mind. That morning Nan Ridley had sent a text to Mitch Arnold. John had not shared the exact wording with her, only that the message indicated Nan had misplaced her clipboard before she'd left for her new position, and she'd messaged to ask Mitch if he'd seen it.

Mitch had responded that he hadn't, and met with John to show him the texts. Further, Mitch had texted Nan that she was considered a "missing person" and to contact the police but had received no reply to his suggestion.

"Can you trace it? Figure out where it was sent from?" Keegan had demanded.

"Technically, we can, given enough time, but…"

"But," Tracy had finished for him, "you don't have enough evidence that a crime has been committed."

The silence spoke volumes. John still didn't believe her, but at least he'd finished his report and left before things had gotten too heated between the two half brothers.

Keegan drove with his fingers tightly clutching the wheel. "What's it gonna take before he believes you?"

"Why would he if there's still no body and not a single soul shouting murder except me?" It made her want to scream.

"Someone's got Nan's phone. Plain as the nose on my face," Keegan grumbled.

"For once, I agree with him," Grandpa Stew said.

They came upon the ranch set in a hollow of hills and bordered by a neat white fence. Keegan came around to the passenger side to help her grandfather from the truck, but he ignored the offered hand and climbed clumsily out. Cyclone bumped a nose against his good leg.

"Nutty dog."

But Tracy noticed his lips twist with amusement as Cyclone headed straight to the pasture fence where a herd of miniature horses cropped at the grass, their withers no more than thirty-five inches high. His tail went into overdrive as he touched his nose to their soft muzzles.

An older woman with her white hair caught in a braid came to meet them. "I'm Lorna Styles. Can I help you?"

Tracy introduced them. "I called you. I wondered if you knew a woman named Nan Ridley."

Lorna opened the gate for them to enter the horse pasture. "Sure. She does some vet care for me once a month." A little black horse trotted up to Lorna and butted her playfully in the hip. The horse's rear hoof was a shiny metallic prosthetic. "She's been great with Buttons here. All our horses are rescues, most from people who don't realize how much work a horse is, no matter the size. Buttons lost a hoof after a dog mangled him. Has a prosthetic now. Nan took real good care of him through the whole process."

"Ain't that something," Grandpa said, peering close. "A

fake hoof. What do you do with these horses? They're too small to do any work."

"We try to find them loving homes, but Buttons is twenty-five, and no one wants an old horse with a bum foot."

Grandpa sighed and patted the horse. "I hear that, little fella. Old rancher with a messed-up knee ain't much in demand, either."

Tracy dropped to her knees and scratched the animal's neck. Buttons snuffled her pockets with a nose soft as velvet. "Wish I had a sugar cube for you, sweetie."

Cyclone circled Buttons, eager to keep him close.

Lorna smiled. "Nan always brings him an extra lump. He's her favorite."

"Have you heard from Nan recently?" Keegan asked.

"No, but I wouldn't expect to. She'll call after the New Year, I'm certain."

Tracy continued to fondle the darling horse, who lipped the edge of her jacket, but her spirits nose-dived. New Year's? How could she wait another three weeks to know if her gut was right, that something terrible had happened to Nan?

Lorna eyed them closer. "Why are you asking all these questions?"

Tracy straightened. "Because I think she's been the victim of a crime."

Lorna's mouth fell open. "The police…"

"The police don't believe me," she hastened to add, "and I have no evidence to prove I'm right."

"I hope you're not. Nan is a good person, committed to doing the right thing, and she never backed down from a fight."

"I hope I'm wrong, too," Tracy said, the feeling of defeat weighing down her limbs. "I pray with all my heart that she is just fine."

They walked back to the truck, Buttons following as far as the fence would allow him, tail swishing and ears swiveling.

"I think he wants you to take him home," Keegan said.

"I sure wish I could, but the stables are a mess and with...well, in light of the fact that someone wants me dead..." Her eyes stung, and this time it was not a lingering reaction to the chemicals that had nearly killed her. He wrapped her in a side hug and her emotions throbbed. She wished she could see some sign of it in him, too, that he felt the same overwhelming connection that she did, but he was all business as they got into the truck.

Keegan turned on the engine and they were headed out along the gravel road when Lorna jogged up, flagging them down.

"I thought of something," she said. "When Nan was last here, about a week ago to check Buttons, she was talking on her cell, and it seemed like an unhappy conversation."

Keegan frowned. "Do you know who she was talking with?"

Lorna shook her head. "I do remember one thing she said, though. It struck me as odd."

Tracy leaned onto Keegan's shoulder to catch every word.

"She said, 'I'm going to get proof. You won't get away with it.'"

Proof? Of a crime that had to be concealed at all costs?

"Is it okay if we pass this along to the police?" Keegan asked.

"If it will help. Anything for Nan."

"Thank you, Lorna," Tracy said before they left the woman behind.

"Proof about what?" she wondered aloud.

"Nan's business was animals. Some sort of mistreatment of the horses? Bulls?" Keegan snorted his disgust. "Anyone who hurts an animal deserves to be punished."

"I agree," her grandfather said. He and Keegan both stared out the window, jaws tight and nostrils flared. At last, they'd actually agreed on two things in one day. Maybe there was hope of a thawing in the hostilities.

"I need to go to the Mother Lode. I can ask questions while I finish evaluating Flight of Fancy."

"No," both men said in perfect unison.

Tracy ground her teeth. Great. Another thing they agreed on. It was time to remind them both that she was an independent woman. "If you won't take me, then let me out of the truck and I'll find my own way there."

Grandpa Stew looked at Keegan. "She's a stubborn one."

"Takes after her grandfather?"

"Maybe, but she ain't gonna back down."

Keegan sighed. "No, that's certain."

"And at least if we take her now, I can look out for her."

"And so can I."

Her grandfather didn't look happy, but he didn't argue. "Fine, then. That's what we'll do."

Tracy folded her arms. "You know I'm sitting squished between you two, right? I can hear every word of you both planning my life for me, deciding how things are going to go."

"Glad you're listening," Grandpa said, "so hear this loud and clear. You're not gonna be running off anywhere in the Mother Lode where we can't clap eyes on you." Her grandfather relaxed against the seat back. "Now that everything's settled, gonna get me a few winks while we drive over there.

Keep us on the road, Thorn. Think you can manage it without running into any gang friends or getting us shot at?"

Keegan turned onto the highway. "I'll try, sir."

Tracy shot Keegan one more exasperated look.

"What?" he said.

"You don't think you're being the tiniest bit bossy?"

"Bossy?" He grinned. "Nah, that's just my natural leadership skills coming out, Pockets."

She would have continued fuming if his grin hadn't made him look like a little boy trying on his father's coat and tie.

She squelched a smile. She'd had to be so strong for such a long time. Maybe it wouldn't hurt for a short while to allow the warmth and concern of two good men to envelop her.

With a soft outward breath, she closed her eyes and snuggled between them.

Keegan spotted the Gold Bar horse trailer as he searched for a spot in the center's parking lot. The Mother Lode was bustling with activity, though the opening ceremony would not take place until six in the evening. His father was supervising the unfurling of a massive canvas sign over the main building, while people unloaded horses and carried saddles and assorted gear into the arena.

As he held the door open for Tracy to hop out, he recognized a guy he'd met, a bull rider he'd admired at other competitions.

"Dex," he said.

The man hefted his saddle over his shoulder and gripped his hand. "Keegan. Gonna ride Outlaw at this show?"

"Yeah. Gonna win with him, too. How are the bulls looking?"

Dex shrugged. "Great, which surprised me. I've ridden

Arnold's bulls before and they haven't performed worth a dollar. He's got 'em kicking just fine now. Couple of us volunteered to do a practice ride, make sure the chutes are working properly and all." He grinned and shot an appreciative glance at Tracy that lasted a second too long. "Gonna come watch? I'm legendary."

Keegan looped an arm around Tracy's shoulders. "Yeah. Legendary in your own mind, Dex."

Tracy smiled at Dex with a warmth that made Keegan inch her closer to him. "We've got some business to attend to."

Dex put a finger to his hat. "All right, then. See you later."

Tracy detached herself from Keegan. "You don't have to speak for me, you know."

"Dex collects female fans wherever he competes. You have to keep a wary eye on him."

She arched an eyebrow. "Don't worry. I'm not susceptible to smooth talkers."

He grinned. "Still mad that I bossed you around?"

"No." She wanted to be, but he was just so impossibly charming, handsome, full of fun, nearly irresistible—if she was being honest. Wrestling her thoughts back to the practical, her smile faded away. "But now that we're here, I want to get my job done and go home." She shivered. "This place gives me the creeps."

"You don't have to—" he started.

"I see Regina. I'm going to ask her if I can ride Flight."

He started in again but she cut him off. "No more bossiness. I won't draw attention to myself or creep into any dark corners, but I have work to do for my client."

"I'm still not a fan of the idea."

"Noted." She sighed. "Anyway, I'm under tight surveillance since Grandpa and Cyclone are tracking me like a stray sheep."

Her grandfather shrugged unapologetically.

Keegan's tension relaxed a fraction. "All right. I'm going to check in with my brothers, then. I'll ask if they've heard anything about Mitch and his bulls."

She frowned. "You think he's mistreating them in some way, and Nan found out? But the text he received from her—"

"Could be he sent them from her phone to fake out the cops. Something about that guy is a burr under my saddle."

She laughed and touched a finger to his chest. "Plenty of things are burrs under your saddle, Mr. Iron Cowboy."

He caught her finger and pressed a kiss to the tip.

She marched away and he admired her graceful stride, the way she was both small and strong at the same time. *I could watch her forever.* The notion made his pulse do a strange flutter kick thing, so he made a pretense of zipping his jacket before Stew could accuse him of ogling his granddaughter.

Stew took a seat on a wooden crate in a position where he could see both Tracy and the bustle of a small herd of cows being backed into a holding pen. Cyclone paced around him, whiskers twitching.

Keegan hastened to his brothers.

The twins, Jack and Owen, were consulting a piece of paper when he joined them. "Back pasture, east. That's where we unload." The six horses they'd brought were in excellent condition and would go for a good price at the auction.

He filled them in on his conversation with Dex about Mitch Arnold.

Owen frowned. "I'll see what I can find out. We're

hanging around to see the bull riding demo, right after we get these horses unloaded."

Jack shifted. "Heard something while I was checking us in."

Keegan waited expectantly.

Owen prodded his twin. "Well?"

"Aw, it's gossip." He looked at his boots. "Hate to spread it around."

That was textbook Jack, the steadiest of the Thorn brothers, a rock with unshakable integrity. Keegan was struck again with how good a man he was, along with Owen and Barrett, and how blessed he was to have been folded into the clan. A quality family, much better than he deserved.

"Not gonna make you do something you're uncomfortable with," Keegan mumbled.

Owen shot him a look of shock and disdain. "Since when? Never mind, don't answer. This is not the time to be Miss Mary Manners, Jack. We need all the intel we can get. Let's have the report ASAP."

Jack's cheeks went ruddy. "Well, the two gals behind me said that Mitch has been married a few times."

Owen jammed his hands on his hips. "Uh-huh…and?"

"And he's currently engaged to Regina Parker."

"So?" Owen was more patient since he'd fallen in love with Ella, but his patience only went so far.

Jack rubbed a hand over his chin. "So, according to the women, he isn't divorced from his last wife, but Regina doesn't know that."

Thoughts tumbled through Keegan's mind. Mitch had a thing for the ladies, so maybe he'd tried his game out on Nan? She'd rejected him and he'd killed her?

Or Regina had discovered them and committed the murder herself?

Fear amped up another notch as he considered a different angle. What if Regina and Mitch were in on the murder together?

Whether it made him look bossy or not, he had to find Tracy.

SIXTEEN

Regina was obviously irritated at Tracy's request to see Flight, but Bryce Larraby interrupted their conversation, smile wide, a whiff of some musky aftershave clinging to him.

"I'm so relieved we've got that Nan Ridley situation resolved."

"We do?" Tracy said.

His smile did not waver. "Of course. The text to Mitch—she's just fine. Whatever you think you saw, it wasn't what you thought. A misunderstanding."

Murder isn't a misunderstanding. Tracy decided the wisest course of action was to swallow her comment and stick to business. "I'd like to take Flight out for a quick ride if I could."

He pursed his lips. "A ride isn't feasible right now with all the hullabaloo around here, but no reason we can't put him in a corral for you to examine. Regina, can you see to that?"

"But I've got a million other duties right now," Regina snapped.

"It will just take a moment. Bring Flight to the east corral if you would." Bryce put a hand on her biceps. The touch seemed to gentle her mood and the look she turned on him was filled with adoration.

Bryce Larraby was charming, no doubt about that. His blue eyes brimmed with warmth, and he was quick with the kind word and considerate gesture, like buying coffee for all his hardworking stable hands.

Thinking about that day at the café made Tracy's throat burn and she swallowed the taste of fear.

He must have read something in her face. "The corral is safe. No hay bales there. I still shudder when I think of how close you came to being seriously hurt." He nodded at Regina. "Please. The horse."

"All right," she said, angry strides conveying her mood.

Bryce sighed. "Unhappy woman. Left a troubled home at fifteen and has fended for herself ever since. She's found a family here at the Mother Lode, maybe even a husband if Mitch treats her well enough."

"You think he won't?"

A wrinkle appeared between Bryce's brows. "Some men take women for granted." He sighed. "And I know that's the pot calling the kettle black. It's taken me a lifetime to learn the lesson. My wife, Marie, is everything to me, and at this ripe old age, I finally figured out that she deserves the best, my stepsons, too."

Tracy followed his gaze as he watched Keegan talking to his brothers. "I was a slow learner and it cost me dearly. I just hope Mitch figures it out sooner than I did. John, too, though he hasn't gotten around to finding a woman yet."

The words came out before she could filter them. "Do you regret what happened with Keegan?"

He started as if she'd struck him. "That was a mistake."

"No," she said. "A child, a little boy—your little boy."

He looked at her, shadows shifting in his eyes, and she could not read him. Was it regret she saw there? A desire to change things with his son? Or was it annoyance that she'd pulled him into embarrassing waters? But she did not regret her harsh statement. Learning from mistakes didn't mean you got to walk away from the devastation. Her father had accepted the consequences for his actions and, by default, so had she. Keegan and his mother deserved better.

Someone called to Bryce. "Mayor Larraby, a reporter wants a minute. Can you oblige?"

He straightened. "Duty calls. Big day. I will talk to you later, Miss Wilson."

"Tracy," she corrected, but he was already striding off, smile wide and beaming geniality, all sign of struggle smoothed over. The perfect mayor, an excellent face for the Mother Lode. So hard to believe he'd lived anything but an exemplary life.

Regina led Flight into the corral, stroking a palm tenderly over his sleek neck. "You're a good horse, aren't you?" she said. "If I had the money, I'd buy you myself."

"Thank you, Regina, for bringing him. You're great with the horses. It must be so nice for Bryce to have you here."

She lifted a shoulder. "Anyway, I'll come get him when you're done."

"Can I ask you one question before you go?"

Her eyes narrowed to slits, but she did not turn away. "What do you want to know?"

"Were you surprised that Nan Ridley quit so suddenly?"

At first she thought Regina wasn't going to answer. But then she spoke. "Actually, yes. I mean, I didn't like her much, but I could tell she was a good vet, good with the horses and bulls. Even took care of the barn cat when he needed some stitches. I like people like that—you know, who value what everyone else thinks is unimportant."

"I do, too." She took in Regina's frizzy braids, the hat

she kept pulled down low on her forehead, and it occurred to her that Regina was a woman who had probably felt unimportant plenty of times in her life. She sought something to say that would build a bridge between them. "Your earrings are pretty."

Regina fingered one as if she'd forgotten they were there. "Mitch gave them to me for my birthday. Never got a gift of jewelry before. Antiques, he said."

"They suit you."

"Thanks. Anyway, um, I'll return the horse when you're done."

Tracy thanked her again and approached Flight.

They'd spent only a few minutes together before a stable hand opened the gate and ushered three other horses into the corral. They were spirited, and one, obviously the dominant of the group, hastened over to Flight, ears pinned, pushing his nose at the stallion. Flight danced back a few steps and Tracy knew it was time to correct the situation, which might become unsafe for her and the horses at any moment. She led Flight out of the space and her grandpa met her.

"I'm going to ride him along the trail there." She pointed to a path bordering a wooded edge of the sprawling property.

"No," Grandpa said. "You're not to be anywhere out of my sight."

"I won't be out of your sight," she said, shoving her hair back. "I'll ride him just to the storage shelter, and you can see me the whole time." At that moment two other riders ambled along the path, headed back to the barn.

"See? Plenty of people around."

"I'm still not—"

She cupped his cheek and kissed him on the forehead.

"Grandpa, I'm going to do my job. If I stop, we'll never get the campground up and running."

His hard expression softened. "Won't be worth a plug nickel if anything happens to you."

She kissed him again. "Nothing will, not during a short ride with you watching my every move."

"Just in case, take Cyclone with you."

She swung up on the horse and Cyclone pranced around Flight's hooves. They started out along the path.

Out of the corner of her eye she saw Keegan straighten, heading right for her grandfather as he noticed her riding away.

Protective, just like her grandpa. It warmed her, just like his kiss, his caress, the maddening way he bossed her around sometimes, as if he were not just a friend, but so much more.

More? Could she even imagine opening herself up to such vulnerability at this time with a man like Keegan? She had not known him long, yet he'd become braided around her heart, twined in her every thought. But she'd decided to go it alone, hadn't she?

Little butterflies jumped in her stomach as Flight walked along. She could tell he was enjoying the feel of the winter sun on his back, the smell of the oak leaves and the crunch of grass under his hooves. She breathed in deep, feeling the smooth gait of the horse, his strong muscles bunching under her fingers as she stroked his neck with her free hand. With each easy step of the stallion, she let go of her concerns—Nan, the campground, Keegan—and enjoyed the respite.

They made it to the storage shelter in fifteen minutes. Both relaxed and easy, they approached the three-sided wooden structure, which sheltered some stacked crates, buckets of nails and an assortment of horseshoes. Cyclone pranced ahead, sniffing the stacks with enthusiasm.

She allowed Flight to crop some grass that had managed to hold on to its green through the long, dry months until the winter storms began to revive it. Stomach growling, she wished she'd brought a snack, too. Keegan probably had something edible in his pockets, an idea that made her smile. Looking back toward the center, she could see him there, standing next to her grandfather, hands on hips, silhouetted by the noontime sun. If they didn't get back soon, he'd commandeer a horse and following, or set out on foot.

Again, she felt a surge of warmth when she looked at Keegan.

But whatever she felt for him was no more than girlish fancy, and one-sided at that.

"Better get back," she said to Flight, urging him away from the grass and pointing his nose in the direction of the center.

"Come on, Cyclone."

The dog went on alert, ears erect, tail high and the scruff of his neck raised.

At first her breathing stopped as she pictured the faceless murderer returned to choke her, the stuff of her nightmares, but there was no one hiding in the shelter among the boxes and detritus. The space wasn't big enough for someone to hide, she told herself sternly, and no one had known of her plans to ride, not even she until a few moments before.

Relax, Tracy. The dog was after a rat or something.

"Cyclone," she said sternly. "Let's go."

But the dog pawed at the bottom crate, working at a crack in one of the slats.

"Cyclone, I mean it," she snapped. The dog persisted.

"Fine." She slid off the horse. "But I hope you realize that Keegan is going to charge over here now like John Wayne. Come on, Cyclone." She reached for his collar. Her fingers just skimmed his silky hair when Cyclone succeeded in pawing loose the small section of broken wood.

Tracy's blood turned to ice as she saw a face between the slats, frozen in death, staring back at her with sightless eyes.

"Unbelievable," Keegan said as he watched Tracy poking around the storage area while Flight stood nearby. "What does she think she's playing at?" His anger turned to fear as she suddenly turned, leaped onto the horse and urged Flight to a gallop, tearing up the distance to the center, Cyclone flying along at their heels.

"What?" he shouted as she reined in the horse and tied him quickly to the fence. Her mouth was tight with horror and he grabbed her as she nearly collapsed in his arms.

"What's wrong?" Grandpa Stew asked, trying to quiet Cyclone, who was barking now at an earsplitting volume.

"It's her." Tracy swallowed convulsively. "It's Nan Ridley. Her body."

Keegan's mouth went dry. "Where?"

"The…the storage shelter," Tracy said.

Keegan helped her to sit next to her grandfather on the crate. "Stay here. I'll check it out." Keegan eyed Stew. "Can—"

He didn't get any more words out before the shouting started behind him. Some spectators who had arrived early for the opening ceremony erupted from the event center, screaming and running in all directions.

Jack and Owen, ropes in hand, raced toward him, and at first he could not understand what in the world had caused the panic, until he saw the bucking bull charging out of the open doors.

The massive animal was running loose, hind end flailing, followed by a second, snorting his rage and heading right for them.

SEVENTEEN

The bulls charged in wild circles, kicking and bucking out their violent rage. The biggest one lowered his horns and charged toward Tracy and her grandfather. Her legs were still shaking so badly she could not run away if she'd wanted to.

The eyes... Nan's eyes...staring, her crumpled form packed into a crate...

"Everybody into the barn!" Jack shouted.

Still she could not make her legs obey, but Keegan scooped her up and raced with her into the barn, away from the stampeding hooves. Owen untied Flight and handed him over to a stable hand, who ran him out of harm's way.

"Grandpa!" she cried.

"I'll get him," Keegan said, running back out through the chaos.

She saw Owen swinging a lasso on one side while Jack did the same on the other. Keegan returned in a moment, half carrying Grandpa and propping him next to Tracy. Cyclone barked twice and ran outside, yelping and racing circles around Jack, Owen and the two bulls.

Keegan grabbed a rope from a peg on the wall and ran toward the second bull. Whirling a rope above his head, he tossed it at the horns of the creature, missing by inches.

The bull charged toward him, saliva dripping from its muzzle, leaping, twisting as if trying to dislodge a rider from his back. Tracy screamed. The animal's horns were kept dull for safety, but they would still plunge through human flesh easily with fifteen hundred pounds of muscle and rage behind them.

Keegan barely managed to hurtle over the corral fence, and the bull crashed into the metal with a ferocious clang before dancing away. Had Keegan been gored? Her angle didn't give her a good enough view. After what seemed like an eternity, he got to his feet and relief poured through her.

Hands pressed to her mouth, she watched.

"He'll be okay," Grandpa said, squeezing her shoulders. "He knows his animals. Works with them every day."

Not bucking bulls, she thought, not like these.

Keegan climbed back over the fence and readied the rope for a second try, letting out the length a little at a time.

Jack and Owen had already snared their ropes around the first bull's neck. Though the animal was still fighting madly, the two men were joined by four more who hauled on the ropes, gradually pulling the bull toward an empty corral.

Keegan finally lassoed the second bull, which spurred the animal into a frenzy of kicking. Hooves slashed toward Keegan, and Tracy screamed again.

The bull smashed through a wooden bench with one vicious spin and kick. Bits of wood flew through the air. Keegan ducked and darted without losing his grip on the rope. Finally, Jack and Owen and the rest of the men came and added another rope and their combined body weight. The second bull was slowly forced into the pen with his companion, and the gate locked behind them.

The area filled with people as everyone came out of their hiding places. It was a good ten minutes more of chaos as spectators and stable workers milled around, righting chairs and checking the animal pens to be sure nothing else had been left open.

"What happened?" Grandpa demanded. "How did those animals get loose?"

Jack was still breathing hard as he approached with Owen. "Dunno. One minute he's in the holding pen ready for the chute, and the next he's out, along with his buddy."

"Someone let them out," Owen said. "That's clear."

Mitch and Regina came running.

"Who let my bulls loose?" Mitch roared. "Did you hurt them? Roping them like that?"

"Nice of you to finally check in. You could have come earlier to help contain them." Keegan dusted off his jeans and joined his brothers, wiping at the sweat on his brow. "Someone let your bulls out on purpose, and they're fine, which is more than any victims would have been if your bulls had tossed them."

Mitch glowered at Keegan and his brothers. "These animals are precious. They've cost hundreds of thousands to raise into champions. If you hurt them at all..."

Regina touched his arm, but he shook her off.

"They didn't," she railed. "The bulls are fine. Quit mouthing off."

"They'd better be," he said. "Or I'm holding these cowboys responsible."

Keegan seemed to grow in height, anger bridling in his expression. "Your animals could have killed someone, and we prevented that, so back off, Mitch."

Mitch lurched forward. "I don't take orders from you or any other man."

Keegan's stare bored into him. "I'm not gonna tell you twice."

Mitch faced him, hands fisted.

"Enough," Bryce Larraby barked, hastening over. Sweat glistened on his forehead. They both turned to stare at him. "It was an accident. The animals aren't hurt. Keep your voices down, and let's have some order around here."

Keegan stared at his father. "Accident. Another one? You're not seriously going to try that line again, are you?"

"Keegan," Bryce said, cheeks flushed, breath coming fast. "You're not going to ruin this day."

"I would think the three thousand pounds of angry bull on the rampage would have already done that," Keegan snapped.

Bryce's mouth tightened into an angry line.

"Stop," Tracy said.

Everyone turned to look at her. Heat flooded her face, and with every fiber in her, she wanted to run. She was not sure she had the courage to put her terrible knowledge into words.

But there was a body...

A young woman whose life had been stripped away...

A woman with a bright future, who noticed the unimportant creatures and worked to help them.

"I found Nan Ridley's body," she whispered.

Now Bryce's eyes went round. "What?"

Mitch blew out a breath. "Are we back to that again?"

"There," she said, pointing a shaking finger at the storage shelter. "In a crate. The dog, Cyclone, sniffed it out when I was riding Flight. It's Nan. I remember now, for sure. She's the victim I saw being strangled."

"By whom?" Mitch asked, his tone rich with sarcasm. "Can you at least put a name to the murderer?"

Tears threatened again, but she blinked hard. This was about justice for Nan, and she would not allow her own feelings to get in the way. "No. Not yet."

Bryce drew close and wiped at his forehead. "Please,

Miss Wilson. This is our opening day, and these bulls were already enough of a problem. I beg of you to not add any more difficulties. I'm sure you're mistaken about what you saw." His gaze flicked to the collective crowd.

Keegan started to blurt something out, but Tracy silenced him with a grip on his wrist.

"Mr. Larraby, Nan Ridley's body is in a crate on your property. That's all that matters now, more than your show or anything else."

He stared at her, inscrutable. "Miss Wilson…"

"Please," she said, not caring if she sounded like she was a raving lunatic. "You have to come with me, right now."

Bryce huffed out a breath and turned, beaming a smile at the crowd. "Well, what's a horse show without a little excitement?" he called out. "At least we know the bulls will be great competitors this year, huh? And how about those cowboys in action? You're getting your ticket money's worth, aren't you?"

There were a few nervous twitters from the crowd and even a smattering of laughter. Tracy saw a bead of sweat glistening on Bryce's upper lip and dark circles staining the armpits of his shirt. It was the first time she'd seen him rattled. He looked as though he might have a heart attack.

"Very sorry for the running of the bulls, but everything is on track for the opening ceremony in…" He consulted his watch and his hand shook. "An hour exactly. Feel free to go stake out a good spot in the arena. I'll arrange for free drinks and popcorn at the concession stand."

With an excited murmur, the crowd began to disperse back to the arena. Bryce moved close to Tracy. "All right. We'll go look at the crate, but everyone doesn't need to know about it, do they?"

She gathered her sweater around her, stomach quivering at the thought of what she had to look at again. With her chin up, she took a few trembling steps in the direction of the shed, following Mitch, Regina and Bryce.

Keegan cupped his palm under her elbow, and she did not try to brush off the support. His strength, his steadfastness was the only thing holding her upright.

"John is on his way. You don't have to do this," he murmured. "I'll take care of it. You stay with Grandpa Stew."

She blinked hard. "I need to."

"Why, Pockets?"

His soft tone nearly made her sob as she tried to find the words. "I feel like…like we're connected somehow, Nan and I. I was there when someone ended her life and she… I mean… I'm responsible for seeing that she gets justice."

"That's a lot of weight on your shoulders."

She managed a wan smile. "I can take it. I…" Suddenly a lump formed in her throat. "I helped my father pass from this life to the next, and I can do the same for Nan. I don't look like it, but I'm strong."

His gaze was filled with such warmth and admiration, it almost made her start blubbering right then and there.

"Yes, you are," he whispered, and he pressed a kiss to the top of her head.

Somehow they made it to the storage shelter. Cyclone barked and beelined to the same spot as before. Tracy swallowed hard against the bile in her throat. "It's the one with the broken slat."

Mitch and Regina pressed in, scanning the sides of the crates.

Bryce peered over their shoulders.

After a moment Regina straightened. "There isn't one with a broken slat."

"There," Tracy said, breaking from Keegan's grasp to point to the correct spot. Only she couldn't.

There was no crate with a broken slat.

The container that had been Nan Ridley's coffin was gone.

EIGHTEEN

Everyone's gaze shifted to Tracy as John Larraby joined them. Keegan clutched Tracy to his side, fearing that her knees would give out.

"Cyclone's sniffed out something," he said. "The crate must have been moved."

John clicked his pen until Keegan wanted to break it in two.

"Did you see anybody doing so? Moving the crate?" John asked.

"No," Keegan admitted, "but I wasn't looking."

"We were busy with a couple of loose bulls." Owen's eyes narrowed. "Convenient timing, wouldn't you say? Those bulls getting loose before Tracy could get help?"

Mitch snorted. "Oh, yeah. That's a diversion now? Maybe we should call it like it is. This woman is wacka-doodle. She's showed up blabbing about a murder, only there wasn't one, and now we're supposed to believe there was a body, but there's nothing here."

"Back off, Mitch," Keegan said.

"No, you back off. We put a lot of money and time into the Silver Spurs show, and this girl has tried her best to ruin it for some reason. Maybe she's looking for a payoff or maybe she's just crazy, but I'm done with the whole thing."

Keegan let go of Tracy. "I'm not gonna let you talk about her like that."

Mitch pulled back a fist and punched Keegan in the cheek. The impact rocked him backward a couple of steps but he was up in a moment, ready to go after Mitch, but his brothers each grabbed him by an arm.

"Easy, Keeg," Owen warned.

Bryce and Regina restrained Mitch.

"All right," Bryce said. "I'm sorry to have to say this, but I really think you need mental help, Miss Wilson. I understand you've suffered a loss recently. John says your father…"

Tracy bent slightly at the waist as if she was in pain. "Please, don't say any more."

"All right. I have to get back now. We've got an opening ceremony to conduct and a horse show to run, and I don't want one more lick of trouble." He released Mitch and nodded to John. "If you need anything else from me, you know where to find me, son."

Son. Keegan bit back the angry tirade that was itching to burst forth. He shook his brothers off and went to Tracy, but she waved him away.

"Tracy."

Her eyes gleamed with a harsh light, mouth tight. "Please," she whispered. "I just want to go home. That's all."

Keegan looked at John, who nodded. "I'll follow up for a statement, but it can wait awhile."

Keegan knew John probably agreed with Mitch that Tracy was crazy, but he appreciated the leeway to get her out of there. They walked slowly back to the truck where Grandpa Stew was waiting.

"What? Did you find her? Is it over?"

Tracy tried to speak but nothing came out, so he helped her into the truck and quickly filled Stew in.

Stew's eyes widened. "What sort of game is this?" he murmured. "Who could have moved a corpse?"

Keegan's eyes roamed the gathering. Who had been close by to hear Tracy's discovery? Someone strong who could have let out the bulls and moved the crate in the time it took to secure the animals, maybe loaded it into a vehicle? Or perhaps it had been two people working together?

Bryce Larraby.

Mitch Arnold.

Regina Parker.

Any of the stable hands.

As he helped Grandpa Stew in beside her, Keegan saw his father take the dais in the outdoor amphitheater, the guests seated on hay bales to watch his talk.

Bryce gestured to a slender woman, striking and stylish, hair short and sleek, and two neatly groomed teen boys, who joined him on the stage. Bryce curved an arm around the woman's shoulders. "I'd like to introduce you to Marie and our two sons, Danny and Clark, the lights of my life."

Keegan watched John, who stood with arms folded, listening.

Two sons. The lights of my life.

As the phrase echoed, John turned away, walking to his squad car.

Welcome to my world, Keegan thought, and he wanted to revel in the fact that his half brother understood what rejection felt like. John deserved to suffer for all the misery he'd heaped on Keegan, the constant reminders that John was accepted and Keegan was not. Instead, as he watched John walk to his car with slumped shoulders, he experienced only a hollow sensation in his gut. Sorrow perhaps, or regret, Bree might have labeled it, but to him it felt like an endless ride to a place he no longer wanted to go.

The laughter of the crowd rose and fell as they hung upon Mayor Bryce Larraby's every word. Loose bulls and lost corpses would do nothing to derail Bryce's meticulously planned event. The mayor, the small-town benefactor, a father figure to the whole town would set things right. When the darkness in Keegan's heart threatened to choke him, he jammed his hat down on his brow.

You'll have your chance later, Keegan. Take care of Tracy. He got behind the wheel and took the road out of town.

Tracy was silent, staring at her fingers twisted together in her lap.

Grandpa Stew shot him a questioning look.

He shook his head. *I don't know what to say, either.*

After a moment he cleared his throat. "How about we stop at the Gold Bar? I—"

"No," Tracy said. "I want to go home."

The way her voice trembled when she said it, barely a whisper, made his gut hitch. "Okay."

By the time they reached the lonely property in the foothills, he prayed that he'd figure out something, anything, to break through the wall of shock and grief that now stood between them.

"There's no danger anymore," she said when he unlocked the cabin door and ushered her inside. Grandpa headed to the kitchen and began to rattle the coffeepot. "I've been proven crazy in front of everyone. Maybe I am crazy."

He gripped her arms. "No, you're not. You saw Nan Ridley murdered, and someone at the center is hiding the truth."

"That's what you want to believe," she said, eyes burning. "Because you want to see your father brought low."

"Not true."

"Yes, it is." Tears glimmered in the weak light. "I can see it in your face when you look at him with more passion than you..."

Look at me? Why did he have the feeling that was how she meant to complete the sentence?

"Tracy, what I feel for you is... I mean, I..."

"What?" Her hazel eyes demanded an answer. "What is there between us besides your need to protect me and punish your father?"

He did not know how to answer. Confusion warred with affection, devotion, angst, fear and everything in between. He thought they'd had an understanding, but now he felt as if he understood nothing. All the words got tangled up inside his mouth, so he did the only thing he could think of. He pressed his lips to hers and kissed her long and slow. She kissed him back, tenderly, so sweetly it both broke his heart and mended the jagged pieces together in that one delicious moment in time. It felt so wonderful, so unlike anything he'd ever experienced, that he drew back so he would not be lost in it altogether.

What was she to him? A means to an end? A woman who needed protecting? A woman who'd roped his heart? The kiss left him unable to come up with a single answer.

The kiss was warm comfort, a balm to her ache, and Tracy let herself feel it in every cell of her body until he pulled away. Her breathing was uneven as she stayed close to him for a minute more until her doubts intruded again.

He did not want to have a relationship with her, not in the way she needed. Ulterior motives, as her grandpa would say. How the knowledge burned, but it was a pain to indulge later. Now was not the time to let her defenses down. She moved away, fighting for calm, and Keegan cleared his throat as her grandpa returned. "Coffee'll take a few minutes."

She nodded and the room fell into painful silence. She felt the worried glances from both her grandpa and Keegan, but she could not bring herself to meet their eyes. Her mind was a numb void, thoughts whirling like startled birds that could not land anywhere, the warmth of his kiss fading away into that dark abyss, too.

She did not know how much time had passed until she found herself deposited on the sofa with a mug of hot coffee in her hand, which Grandpa Stew had prepared while Keegan lit a fire to warm the cold cabin. She watched Keegan's back. Had she really shared a kiss with him, or was her mind making up things now to fill in the gaps in her ragged memory? But the tingling of his lips on hers remained, the only spot of comfort, which was certainly what he'd intended. *Comfort, protection, justice...but not love. Not that.*

Grandpa fussed around, straightening things and making them even more crooked, restacking the kindling pile only to knock it more askew.

"It's okay," she told him. "I'm okay. I just need to think this out for a minute."

He looked dubious. Cyclone paced around his legs, feeling his uncertainty.

"Why don't you take Cyclone and see what you think about the fencing?" Keegan said. "Needs refitting in a few places, but the stable looks sound enough with some roof repairs. Can be ready in no time."

"Ready for what?" Grandpa huffed.

Keegan arched an eyebrow. "Horses, of course. You can't have a horse camp until you get horses. Gonna need to get 'em settled in and used to the property before you start bringing in the little campers. Sooner the better, in my opinion."

Her dream of a family camp seemed like a distant memory, but Grandpa nodded and let himself out, Cyclone dancing at his crutches.

Keegan eased next to her on the sofa and took her hand. "Like ice," he said, massaging some warmth back into it. He didn't press her to talk, just sat, warming her, steadying her.

Was this what love was like? The thought startled her. Bearing one another's burdens quietly, without even needing to speak? She held on, tears crowding her vision. But this love was one-sided, she reminded herself, a flimsy daydream. Her path was hers alone. She'd be wise to remember that.

"Keegan," she managed to say at last. "Am I crazy?"

"No crazier than anyone else I know," he said. His smile faded. "Tracy, I believe you saw Nan's body."

"No one else does. They all looked at me like…" She swallowed hard. *All those eyes, all that judgment.*

"No one has seen or heard from Nan Ridley since the night you saw her murdered," he said firmly. "She's dead, you found her body, and someone hid it. Someone at the center, familiar with the area, maybe a couple of people working together—one let the bulls loose and one snatched the crate."

"It sounds far-fetched. Impossible."

"John said he's going to ask the Copper Creek cops to bring in a cadaver dog, but that might take a while." Keegan snorted. "They'll try to keep a low profile to protect the event, no doubt."

"They might not find anything by then."

"Dogs are amazing. They might still alert that there was a cadaver in the storage shelter."

"But with no body to be found, there's no proof. We're back to square one." She looked around helplessly. "What should I do? All these plans. I put every last penny into this place. How can I stay here when people think…?" She gulped. "It may never come out what really happened to Nan that night."

"Pockets," he said, pressing a kiss to her palm, "I'm not going to give up until we know the truth. In the meantime…" He looked around. "You should carry on with your dreams, build that horse camp and take care of your rascally grandfather." He said it like it was the most obvious statement in the world.

She stared at him, overwhelmed by the kindness, the steadfastness, his belief in her dream. When he put a hand behind her neck and pulled her in for another kiss, she did not resist. She would accept his comfort, if that was all he could give her, and offer her love, though it was a gift he did not want.

The comfort in that joining was so precious, so tender, that the tears flowed unchecked down her cheeks. He kissed her once more and then wiped a thumb along her face to catch them.

Love circled and frolicked in her heart. How her feelings had shifted from friendship to something much deeper, she could not pinpoint, but that kiss kindled something inside she could not deny. Whatever else happened, she knew Keegan would be in her soul forever. The secret both thrilled and pained her.

He smiled, tugged playfully at a strand of her hair. "Like I said, it's gonna be okay."

They heard her grandfather coming noisily up the walk, purposefully making a ruckus, she suspected. She did not know exactly when Grandpa had switched from loathing Keegan to possibly respecting him, but she didn't care much when the transformation had occurred, only that it had.

Maybe somehow she could keep the friendship of this good man, if she could not have his love. The fullness of her heart forced the horror of the day back, one stuttering beat at a time.

Keegan stood and headed to the door to open it for Grandpa. On the way he scanned the dreary room. "Know what, Pockets? This place needs something."

"It needs a lot of things," she said, brushing her sleeve across her face.

Grandpa stamped in, cheeks reddened with the cold.

Keegan continued to gaze around the dim space.

"I've got an idea," he said, a mischievous gleam in his eye.

Grandpa sat heavily. "Uh-oh. That's gonna be trouble."

Keegan gave both of them a wink. "Trust me," he said. "I'll be back in a jiffy."

NINETEEN

Keegan discussed his plan to surprise Tracy. Jack and Owen loaded up his truck with supplies, offering help when their ranch duties allowed. Barrett would typically be the lead on such matters, but he was distracted, his normally perfect beard untrimmed and a bit of wildness showing around his mouth.

"Doc says it will be soon, anytime now," he said for the third time. His coffee sat ignored on the kitchen table while he drummed his fingers over and over until Owen told him to knock it off.

"It's going to be okay," Ella said, squeezing him around the shoulders. "Mama knows how to take care of Betsy, and I will be there with Shelby if the baby comes while you're away for any reason. She's got my cell and everybody else's."

"Right." Barrett still looked dazed. Keegan understood it was not just first-time-father jitters. He'd lost Bree in the most violent, unexpected way, and he would likely never fully trust that Shelby, too, might not be stripped from him in a moment. God had enabled Barrett to open his heart to another woman, and Keegan would always be in awe of that, but fear lingered somewhere down deep in his brother.

Keegan squeezed Barrett's shoulder. "Hey, man. With

all of us around, we'll get her to the hospital faster than an ambulance could."

Barrett toyed with his mug. "Uh-huh. But Doc says her blood pressure is high. I told him she should be admitted, but he didn't listen."

"No, a doc probably isn't going to take advice from a cowboy," Jack observed.

Barrett got up. "I'm gonna go check on her. She sleeps best in the afternoon. I made her promise not to get up at all while I was gone, but I'm not sure she always does what I say."

Evie and Ella laughed at that one. "What a news flash," Ella said.

"Okay, go check on her, Barrett, but don't wake her," his mother cautioned. "She says she can't get a moment's sleep with you prowling like a panther."

But Barrett was already out the door.

His mother handed Owen a box. "This goes to the barn. Candles for the ceremony. I'm going up to the attic to find the bassinet, just in case that baby shows up tonight."

Owen quirked a smile. "Yes, ma'am."

Ella kissed Owen. "I have to give Betsy her medicine."

"A double wedding and a baby," Jack said after the women left. "Mama's over the moon."

Keegan realized Owen was studying him. "Got something you need to get off your chest?"

Owen's stare, always intense unless he was with Ella, sharpened. "Sonny B's still in town, looking to settle a score with you."

Keegan shrugged. "I've got wilder horses to rope."

"Do you? I would think that after what happened… it being so public and all, Tracy wouldn't want anything more to do with the show or the center."

He squared up with his brother. "A murder happened.

That's not going away no matter how much dear Daddy wants it to."

Something flickered across Owen's face.

"You have to believe that, Owen. Someone has tried to kill Tracy repeatedly."

"Or you."

Keegan straightened. "Explain."

"The car accident, the motorcycle on the property—John's right, those could have been Sonny B looking for you."

Keegan gaped. "So you're taking John's side here?"

"Not anybody's side, just pointing out possibilities."

He shoved a hand through his hair. "Are you forgetting that someone tried to kill her at the café? And somebody let loose the bulls at just the right time?"

"She has enemies, no doubt. I'm just saying that you don't know her well enough to grasp the whole story. You only just met. John's doubts could have some merit, and you shouldn't discard them just because of the bad blood between you. It's possible someone is after her for a different reason, something you know nothing about."

Keegan rocked back on his heels, stunned. "Now you're saying she's a liar?"

"No."

Keegan stared him down. "I thought you had my back, Owen."

"I do, I always will, but this isn't about you against your birth family."

"I know that. It's about Tracy."

Owen folded his arms across his broad chest. "If you believe that, if you care about her, then you'd be willing to step back and look objectively as John suggests. That's the best thing for Tracy, too, isn't it?"

Anger hummed so loud it nearly deafened him. "Owen,

I don't have to explain myself to you. I'll do things my way."

Owen sighed. "Always have."

He almost choked on the words. "You sound just like my half brother," he grated out through gritted teeth.

Jack edged closer. "Owen's watching your back, Keeg. That's all."

"That's not what it feels like. What about you, Jack? Do you think Tracy is crazy and I'm just in this for revenge?"

Jack was silent a moment. "I'm not sure what the truth is, but I know your past is playing into your present."

Keegan fought to push the words out past the betrayal. "I guess I know where you stand now, too."

"Keegan, it's not—" Jack started to explain, but Keegan slammed out of the kitchen, breath coming in angry spurts. He stood for a moment in the late-afternoon sun, but he felt nothing but the cold all the way down to his boots.

So Owen also thought Keegan was blindly trying to defy John and find some dirt on the center? And Jack? The brother he'd thought was closer than blood? His ally no matter what?

The arrow lodged deep in his heart, in a place he'd believed had callused over long ago. He remembered so clearly the feeling of being alone the day his mother died, alone in the bedroom at the ranch house, also on a winter afternoon. And then again when he'd heard that Bree had been killed. Mother, sister, father, half brother, separated by oceans he could not cross. Fists clenched, he wanted to shout, to rage aloud at all the darkness that brimmed inside him.

Instead he sucked in a breath, looked up at the frigid sky and let his will harden into cement.

Fine. If no one would support him and believe Tracy, he'd take care of things all on his own.

His mother called from the front porch. "Keegan?"

He could hear the puzzlement in her voice, the worry, but he could not turn back. Gunning the engine, he drove away, the soft Christmas lights glimmering in his rearview mirror as he left the ranch behind.

Tracy roused herself to make a pot of vegetable soup as the sun slipped toward the horizon. She could not manage to get the oven working, so she prepared corn bread in a cast-iron pan on the stovetop instead. Probably nothing close in quality to Evie's cooking, but it was edible.

Keegan bustled about outside, hammering and sawing. When the soup and biscuits were done, she let herself outside.

Keegan looked up from his sawhorse, a couple of nails in his mouth.

"What are you working on?"

"Patching the stable roof," he mumbled. "Gotta get it in shape for the horses."

Her heart swelled. "Keegan, thank you so much, but I can't let you do all this for me. We can…"

He took the nails from his mouth. "And I worked on one other side project."

She turned to follow his finger. Alongside the porch was a four-foot pine tree, affixed with a crude wooden stand. Under it was a box of ornaments and a neatly coiled string of lights.

"A…Christmas tree?"

"Yes, ma'am. No offense, Pockets, but your place is completely lacking in Christmas cheer. Time to get that ironed out."

Her eyes brimmed. "I didn't have the heart to get one. Dad died just after Christmas last year."

She hadn't realized he had come close, embracing her from behind, pressing his cheek to hers.

"I never met your daddy, but I know he would want you to have Christmas, whether he was around or not."

"Yes, he would."

He kissed her temple and grabbed hold of the tree. "Better get this inside before dark. Can you open the door?"

They crossed the threshold and, quite suddenly, the dank cabin became cozy, comforting and filled with a joy that had been lacking only moments before. The scent of pine mingled with the smell of simmering soup. Grandpa muttered under his breath, but he held the box of ornaments for Tracy to attach after Keegan got the lights twined around the branches.

"Battery powered," Keegan said, "in case you want to turn them on when the generator's not running."

When it was done, they stood back to admire the twinkling wonder. Tracy excused herself and retrieved a box from the storage room, unwrapping the glass ornament hand painted with a starlit manger.

She tried to explain but her throat was clogged with tears.

"Her daddy painted it," her grandfather told him.

Keegan didn't respond and Grandpa didn't complain when he embraced Tracy and caught her tears on his shoulder.

There was such grief and happiness, pain and joy all wrapped together in that one moment.

"Everything's gonna be okay," Keegan breathed into her hair, and for the first time in a very long time, she allowed herself to believe it.

TWENTY

In the icy Wednesday predawn, Keegan drove off on his mission. He knew Tracy, stubborn soul that she was, was intent on going to the horse auction to bid on Flight of Fancy for her client. He was awestruck at how much courage it required for her to return after what she'd seen and how she'd been treated.

Magnificent. He didn't care what his brothers thought. Tracy was nothing short of magnificent, and he intended to stick by her side like glue until she was clear of the horse-center mess for good and vindicated by the truth. No one was going to impugn her reputation and get away with it, especially not anyone with whom he happened to share DNA.

If you have anything to do with this, Dad, you'd better watch out. How supremely satisfying it would be to knock his birth father off his pedestal, to make him pay for what he'd done to Keegan's mother, and to show John that he'd been right all along.

But first, he'd decided, he was going to make Tracy smile so wide it would chase all the bad memories away, at least for a while.

He returned to her property just before six, unloaded his surprise and headed into the kitchen to make coffee. Tracy trundled in, in jeans and a sweatshirt, hair mussed from sleep. Gorgeous, he thought. Not polished and fancy like most of the women he'd dated, but pure and light and honest. He'd never felt so eager to please another living soul. His pulse whammed in his throat as he took her outside. She stiffened beneath his guiding hands and doubt crept in.

Had he overstepped? Gone about the grand gesture without enough consideration to her feelings? It would not be the first time Keegan Thorn had gone overboard to impress a lady, making a colossal fool of himself in the process. Why did he care so much now? Was he sending the wrong message? And what message was that exactly? His palms went clammy and his stomach constricted as he took her into the pasture.

"I, uh, got you a Christmas present."

"You didn't have to…" Then she caught sight of Buttons and another miniature brown horse, standing shoulder to shoulder, breath puffed against the morning sky. She blinked. "Buttons?"

"And that's Ducky. They're friends, and Lorna figured they'd be happier together."

"You bought them for me?"

"Sure did. They're gonna be a hit with the kiddos at the camp."

She went dead quiet, mouth pressed in a thin line, arms hugged around herself.

"Uh, stable's all set up so they'll be warm at night, safe from coyotes and all."

He began to get a bad feeling that he'd stepped into a problem of his own making, as the impact of what he'd done hit him. Two animals that required constant care, brought to a property that needed massive work, to a woman whose life was all edges and pieces. *Flowers*, Keegan berated himself. *You could have just gotten her a nice bunch of carnations. That would have cheered her up, wouldn't it?*

Typical. Overblown. Under thought. He began to think of ways he could undo the knot he'd just tied, when she startled him by throwing her arms around him and nearly knocking him over backward. His hat fell to the ground and she pressed her face to his neck.

"I've never had such an amazing present in my whole life."

He clung to her, holding her tight, then twirled her around, and the feeling of her there in his arms, happy, made him wish he could gift her with presents for a very long time to come.

But his brother's words pricked his memory.

Your past is playing into your present.

Was this strange new feeling Tracy awakened in him love? Or merely protectiveness? Was he full of the need to save her and mete out punishment to his father, or was it something else, something that he had never before known with another woman?

It was too soon. Too much. His brain worked to stanch the wild firings of his heart.

Slowly he settled her back to the ground and accepted her beaming smile as his prize. The joy shining behind those hazel eyes about dazzled him from any rational thought.

Get her out of the mess, Keegan. Only then will you be able to see things clearly.

Tracy hustled into the corral and petted her new companions while he watched. The two tiny horses were timid at first, but Tracy put them at ease until they both began to follow her around the corral. He produced a couple of sugar cubes from his pockets, which he gave to her to share with them.

Friends for life. He checked the time, loath to end it. "You're gonna freeze if you don't get on inside. It's getting late."

Her smile faltered. "I almost forgot. What time is it?"

"Seven thirty."

Now the fear returned again, dimming her bliss, and he kicked himself for being the cause. "You don't have..." he began, but she was already closing the gate carefully and talking in soothing tones to the horses.

"Be home soon, babies. You have fun until I get back."

In the cabin, she headed for her room to change clothes.

Grandpa Stew sat at the table drinking coffee. He poked a crutch in Keegan's direction. "Mighty fancy presents you're getting my granddaughter. That some sort of love token or something?"

Keegan's face went hot. "It's something to cheer her up after everything she's been through."

"Presents like that mean a guy's interested. You interested? Or you just leading her along the garden path?"

He gave Grandpa Stew a close-lipped smile. "Sir, I assure you, I have no plans to lead your granddaughter anywhere she doesn't want to go."

"That ain't an answer."

"I...I want to help her. That's all."

Grandpa Stew stared at him, lips pursed. "All right, then," he said finally. The grizzled eyebrows drew together. "Help is what she needs." He glowered. "The only thing she needs, really, and you'd better be on your toes at the auction today."

"Yes, sir," Keegan said, donning his cowboy hat. "You aren't coming along?"

"Don't tell Tracy, but my ankle is throbbing something fierce. Figure since there's a cop stationed there now and she ain't gonna do nothing crazy like riding about the place, she'll be all right."

Keegan grinned. "She forbade you to come, didn't she?"

He huffed. "Yeah. Heard me groaning last night and said if I insisted on coming, she'd hide my crutches. Tough girl."

He laughed. "That's the best kind."

Tracy arrived in the kitchen with a clipboard under one arm. She was wearing a green sweater that teased the emerald from her hazel eyes, jeans and a denim jacket that tied it all together. Her look was professional, but he read the tension in the taut muscles of her neck.

"Okay, Grandpa. Here's the satellite phone Keegan loaned us. It's charged. Do you remember how to use it?"

"Course I do," he said, smacking it on the table. "I'm not a dope."

She kissed him on the brow. "I know, but even smart, tough ranchers need to remember to dial then push the green button."

He grumbled but his lips curved in a smile.

"Take care of Ducky and Buttons, okay?"

"What kind of names are those?"

She arched a brow. "This from a man whose horse was named Mittens."

"He came with that name, and you can't go changing a horse's name. It confuses them."

"Owen texted me that there are two cops stationed at the horse show," Keegan said as they made their way to his truck.

His attempt to soothe her did not seem to work. Only when she stopped to caress Buttons's muzzle as they passed the corral did the joyful flush return to her cheeks.

Presents like that mean a guy's interested.

And he was, interested in helping Tracy and maybe

something more, if he could only see justice served up to Bryce Larraby on a silver platter first.

Your past is playing into your present.

Only for a short while longer. He could feel it. A face-off was coming, and it was about time for him to emerge as the winner.

Pulse kicked into a higher gear, he opened the passenger door and helped Tracy into the truck.

Tracy filed into the arena after receiving her auction materials. She felt like every eye was on her, every mouth whispering about "that delusional girl" or perhaps "the liar." Keegan kept a firm hand on her lower back as he steered her to a spot near the railing. Shelby sat in the row behind, hand resting on her belly. Barrett sat protectively next to her.

Keegan raised an eyebrow and hugged his sister-in-law. "Surprised to see you here."

Shelby rolled her eyes. "I told Barrett if I didn't get out of the house, I was going to throw a hissy fit the likes of which he'd never seen." She grinned. "It worked."

"Yeah, it did," Barrett said, his expression a mixture of amusement and exasperation. "'Cause I can't seem to say no to you."

"We'll have to work on that if this baby is a girl," she said with a laugh.

Across the arena, Jack and Owen scurried back and forth, tending to the Gold Bar horses that would be offered at the auction. They were all beautiful, well-trained animals, and they'd get top dollar, Keegan was sure.

Tracy gave him a puzzled look. "Don't you want to check in with them?"

"Nah. They know what they're doing. They don't need my help." Did he sound like a petulant child? he wondered.

He felt like one. His brothers loved him, no question, but it still rankled that they didn't trust his judgment or motives. The chip on his shoulder wasn't so massive that it blotted out every other good instinct, he wanted to tell them.

Tracy didn't press further and the auction began. Noise from the spectators, bidders and the clang of the gate opening and closing filled the arena. He sat back to watch Tracy do her work. With an air of calm efficiency, she secured Flight of Fancy for her client.

"She's something." Shelby leaned over to whisper in Keegan's ear as Tracy joined them.

"Yes, ma'am."

"I—" She broke off suddenly and Keegan heard her sharp intake of breath as he turned in his chair. "Barrett…"

"Yeah, honey?"

"I need to leave. Now."

"Now?" Barrett's mouth dropped open. "Is it…?"

"It is." Shelby gasped as a contraction hit her.

Barrett was already moving, supporting his wife's arm as Keegan took his place at the other. Tracy instantly moved ahead of them, clearing the way as they struggled along out of the building into the parking lot.

Clutching Barrett, Shelby doubled over, breath coming in spurts.

"Should I call an ambulance?" Tracy said.

"No." Shelby puffed. "We're ten minutes from the hospital. This could go on for hours. Drive me, please."

Sweat rolled down Barrett's face. Wild-eyed, he looked at Keegan. "Is it supposed to hurt this much so soon?"

Neither Tracy nor Keegan had an answer for that.

"Keegan, you need to drive them," Tracy said. "I'll call Evie and Tom."

"I don't want to leave you here alone."

"You can come back for me. I'll stay inside with everyone else. Go," she said as Shelby groaned and clutched her middle.

Barrett grabbed her arms.

"He shouldn't drive," Tracy whispered to Keegan. "He's too scared. It's not safe. You have to."

In fact, Keegan had never seen his big brother look more unnerved. The guy had faced down a killer who'd threatened Shelby in the past, and broken wild horses without working up a sweat, but now he could hardly get a sentence together. Keegan's own stomach was tumbling.

"We should… I mean…are you…?" Barrett stammered as he picked Shelby up and put her into the truck.

Another groan from Shelby had Barrett almost hollering at his brother. "Come on. We gotta get to the hospital right now."

Keegan took Tracy by the shoulders. "I'll tell my brothers. Stay where it's safe. Promise."

"I promise," she said. "Now go."

He ran to the driver's door, praying that Shelby would deliver the baby without complications, but preferably not in the front seat of a truck with two petrified cowboys. As he caught a glimpse of Tracy in the rearview mirror, his mind called out to her.

Keep your promise. Stay safe.

TWENTY-ONE

Tracy hunkered down in the stands, keeping well under the public radar. She'd brought an old baseball cap of her grandfather's, which she'd crammed over her hair as she took in the auction from under the brim. As far as she could tell, it was a huge success. The horses were mostly of excellent quality, the bidders in a generous mood and the transitions as smooth and seamless as they could be.

By the time the crowd broke for intermission, three of the six Thorn horses had sold for a fair price. As the people around her began to filter outside, Tracy let herself be swept along, rather than stay behind in an empty arena. The tower of hay bales she passed on her way out was only half as high as the pile that almost crushed them before, but it still gave her the chills as she moved quickly by.

Now that she'd been proved a nutcase publicly since Nan's body had disappeared, she didn't think the killer would pursue her any further, but he or she might want to hammer in the last nail, since it was possible she might get her memory back.

Outside, the bystanders queued up for coffee, hamburgers and hot dogs, sizzling hot off the grill. She was gradually pushed back toward the office, but she felt no alarm. A uniformed Copper Creek officer stood just outside the office, nodding and smiling.

She realized in that moment that the next time she returned to the horse center, if her business ever took her there, the place would be stripped of Christmas decor. The lights, ornaments and trees would all have vanished. This was the last chance she'd have to see things as they were, to take one last stab at jogging her memory. She owed it to Nan to at least try.

She peeked through the office windows, frosted with stenciled icicles. Plenty of people swarmed about inside, families taking pictures in front of the tree, a receptionist she didn't know chatting with cowboy types turning in their auction information and checking in for the events on the following days. Her body felt leaden, reluctant to take her into the place where her darkest fears had been awakened, but how could she live the rest of her life with a gaping void where her memory of that night should be?

"There won't be any danger if I stay where the people are," she muttered to herself. Though she wished Keegan were with her, his position front and center in her heart frightened her.

A week ago you could take care of yourself. Nothing's changed.

She ignored the thought that sprang to mind. *Everything's changed.* But one thing must not—she could not rely on a gorgeous blue-eyed cowboy to take care of her. If she was going to get her life back, she had to start somewhere.

Pulling open the door, she marched inside. The warmth enveloped her, scented by a crock full of apple cider that the guests helped themselves to. Bryce Larraby had thought of everything. Bryce's wife stood holding a cup of cider in manicured fingers. She exuded class and style, Tracy thought as she chatted with a man and his wife.

"Teens aren't cheap," Marie said. "Danny and Clark used to want Legos, and now they ask for the latest iPhones. It was motorcycles last year."

Motorcycles. Her mind went immediately to the motorcycle that had sneaked onto their property. How easy would it have been for Bryce to borrow his son's vehicle?

She shook away the thoughts. She was being paranoid. Plenty of people had access to motorcycles.

"Expensive," the man across from her agreed.

Marie laughed. "Good thing the horse show's a success. We're looking at Ivy League colleges for the boys pretty soon."

Hmm. Bryce Larraby had a very good motive to cover up anything that would threaten the show's profitability. Was he capable of murder? It depended on the stakes, she decided. And considering the well-dressed Marie and her college-bound sons, the stakes were pretty high for the mayor.

Tracy excused herself and walked to the other side of the lobby where the Christmas tree sparkled. Leaning against the wall, she closed her eyes, picturing again that horrible night. Nan—she was sure it had been Nan—staring at her with pleading eyes that slowly dimmed in her attacker's choke hold.

Tracy remembered the terror in her stomach as she'd run away in blind panic, knocking against the tree, finding the only unlocked door...

Her eyes popped open. The storage room. The memory blossomed in her mind. She'd slammed inside, put a chair under the door handle and climbed out the window. Heart thumping, she recalled a hand grasping her ankle.

Focus on that hand, she told herself. Had they been a woman's fingers? A man's? Was there anything that could help her identify the attacker? A watch? A bracelet?

Nothing. The figure in her memory remained cloaked in darkness.

Swallowing hard, she eased toward the storage room. *Still plenty of people around*, she told herself, *and you're not going in.* The tile squeaked under her feet as she drew close. Startled, she realized the storage room door was ajar.

Fighting paralysis, she poked it with her toe and it swung open a few inches. "Hello?"

The two people inside did not notice her.

Bryce was inches away from Regina. Her face was stricken with a combination of emotions. Rage? Betrayal? Fear?

"I can't believe it," she whispered. "I thought… I mean… I never would have believed…" She held a photo crammed in her clenched fist.

Bryce took her around the shoulders. "Listen to me, Regina."

"No," she said, wrenching away. "I'll never listen to you again."

She caught sight of Tracy in the doorway, sucked in a breath and slammed past Tracy, knocking her back a step.

Bryce started after her but stopped, his body between Tracy and the lobby. She noticed finally how dark the hallway was, how quiet and removed from the festivities.

You're okay, she breathed, edging toward the wall. *All you have to do is scream.* She started to dart past when Bryce grabbed her wrist, his grip crushing.

The whites of his eyes were eerie in the gloom. The same eyes she'd seen strangling Nan?

"Whatever you're imagining, that wasn't what you

think, and I don't want any more trouble out of you," he snarled.

"Let me go. You're hurting me."

"Not until you agree to get out of here and stay out."

"Get your hands off her."

Tracy heaved out a slow breath as Keegan came up next to her and shoved Bryce back.

"This doesn't concern you, Keegan."

"You put your hands on her. That concerns me." Keegan's eyes were cold as stones. Flat. Hard. "What are you so eager to hide?"

"Nothing." His jaw worked as he strove for control. "It's a private matter with Regina."

Mitch strode up. "What's going on? Regina just lit out of here like a spooked calf."

Bryce held up a palm. "Nothing. It was nothing."

Keegan looked to Tracy, waiting.

"I remembered...being in the storage room. I noticed it was open. Regina and Bryce were in there."

"So you decided to eavesdrop?" Bryce snapped.

"I wasn't eavesdropping. Regina's voice was pretty loud."

"What did she say?" Mitch asked.

Bryce tried again to wave him off, but Tracy repeated what she had heard.

"What's that mean?" Mitch asked Bryce.

Bryce smoothed his shirt. "Like I said, it's a private matter."

The cop approached, elbowing his way past Mitch and another cowboy who had joined the group, the bearded one from the café, Tracy remembered with a hint of unease.

"Folks?" the cop asked. "Everything under control?"

Bryce smiled. "Yes. Thank you for checking. Everything is fine. No need for your help, Officer."

The officer did not take the hint. Instead he smiled affably and stayed put until Mitch turned on his heel and left, the bearded man following.

"Mr. Thorn?" the cop said. "May I suggest you and Miss Wilson step outside? Get a breath of fresh air?"

Tracy tugged on Keegan's sleeve, fearful of the ire kindling in him. "Come on. Let's go. Tell me about Shelby."

Keegan took a step toward Bryce. "I know you're hiding something and I'm going to find out what it is."

"You're going to find nothing," Bryce snapped. "No matter how much you harass and cause trouble, you'll never get what you want from me."

Keegan tensed, and it took all Tracy's strength and a slight movement from the cop to force Keegan away.

When they made it outside, the crowd had thinned and she sucked in a deep breath, knees shaking. Heat radiated out of Keegan, the muscles in his clenched jaw jumping.

"I'm calling John," Keegan said once they were in his truck. "I'll ask him to meet us at your property. He's going to listen this time, and he's going to take this investigation seriously."

She did not think what she'd overheard would change John's mind, but Keegan wasn't in a mood to be tangled with, so she left him to his phone call. Seated in the passenger seat, she tried to rub the feeling of Bryce's grip off her wrist. A movement from the side of the building caught her eye.

Tracy saw Regina shove at Mitch with such force he staggered back against the wall as she strode away.

Regina was strong.

And she was a woman who felt she had been wronged.

Had Nan's murderer been a man?

Or Regina Parker?

* * *

Keegan forced his mind away from what had just happened to answer Tracy's questions.

"We got Shelby there safely. They put her into a room, and my parents are on their way."

"Barrett?"

"Pacing like a caged lion until Shelby told him to sit down."

She blew out a breath.

He let the fear flow into words as they began the drive to her property. "Tracy, you started to remember the details."

She blinked at him. "Not much. Not the faces."

"But enough that Bryce knows, Mitch, maybe Regina, some other people who were around. Really, anybody in the office."

Slowly the understanding dawned and her brow puckered. "You think the killer is coming back after me."

"Yes, and I know my father has something to do with it."

"He said it was a private matter, whatever he and Regina were arguing about."

The granite slab of anger slammed down inside him again. "He also said I'd never get what I wanted from him, but he's wrong."

She brushed his hand with her finger, sending tingles shooting through his nerves. "Keegan—"

He wouldn't let her finish. Instead he gunned the engine and headed back to the foothills. It was a long, silent drive, each of them lost in their own thoughts until they reached Tracy's property.

Tracy took a minute to greet Ducky and Buttons, who hustled to the fence to meet her, before she entered the cabin. Cyclone yipped and licked her arm.

"Well, well," Grandpa said. "Safe and sound." His expression changed as a squad car pulled up outside.

John got out and joined them in the kitchen. "I got the *Reader's Digest* version from the Copper Creek officer. Want to tell me the rest?"

Tracy did and he jotted notes, expression maddeningly bland as always.

"Okay. I'll ask around," he said.

Keegan couldn't keep quiet for another moment. "You have to do more than ask around."

John shot him a look. "For your information, the cadaver dogs did alert on something—" he held up a palm "—which may or may not have been a cadaver. They followed the scent to the woods behind the property, but lost it."

"So someone moved the body. Maybe even loaded it into a car and took off," Keegan snapped.

"It's possible."

"It's more than possible." Keegan got up and paced the small space, dislodging needles from the Christmas tree as he brushed by. "We have to find the killer. They know Tracy's starting to remember."

"Who knows?"

"Bryce, for one. You have to see that, surely, unless you're being intentionally obtuse?"

John stood so fast his chair squeaked against the floorboards. "Outside. Right now."

Keegan was only too eager to follow his half brother onto the porch. He didn't waste any time getting to the point. "You have to—"

"I have to do my job, Keegan, and you have to stay out of this investigation."

"Is that what you call this? An investigation? You haven't believed one single thing Tracy has said since the beginning."

"It doesn't matter what I believe or don't. I need proof, not just your half-baked suspicions."

"They're not half-baked."

"Yes, they are, and what's more, they're fueled not by facts but by your personal agenda."

Keegan's hands curved into fists. "Bryce is the likeliest one to have been able to hide a body. He knows every square inch of his property."

"Would you try to think logically for a minute? Why would he kill his veterinarian? What would his motive be when he's got a multimillion-dollar horse show to hype?"

"Nan knew the animals were being mistreated maybe, or perhaps someone was skimming money."

"Lots of theories. You're grasping at straws. You're so desperate to have him guilty."

"He is guilty." Rage washed through Keegan in angry waves that would no longer be contained, rushing like a tsunami. "He turned his back on me, on his responsibility, and on you, too, John. He's made his new wife and kids his whole world. Does he ever look you up? Ever call to chat? Ask you about anything? Contact you or your mother?"

John flinched. "News flash, Keegan. A guy can be a bad father, but it doesn't make him a criminal."

"I'm gonna prove him guilty, as soon as Tracy gets her memory back."

"And what if she doesn't? Did you ever think about that?"

"She will."

"But if she doesn't…are you going to hang around until she does?"

"I will hang around Tracy forever if it means I can prove Bryce Larraby guilty."

As soon as the words left his mouth, he heard the soft exhalation and looked up to see Tracy standing there, holding a coffeepot and a mug, ready to try to soothe things between Keegan and John.

His last words hung in the air.

I will hang around Tracy forever if it means I can prove Bryce Larraby guilty.

After an awkward silence, John cleared his throat. "I'll talk to you later and let you know what I find out." He tipped his hat to Tracy. "Sorry to bother you, ma'am."

Keegan went to her, sick. "I didn't mean it like that."

Her eyes burned and her voice came out in a harsh whisper. "You meant it exactly like that."

"No."

Tears sparked her hazel irises to life. "My grandpa has told me the whole time that you were using me, maybe without even knowing it, but I didn't want to believe him."

The hurt in her eyes cut like a razor. "Tracy, I…"

"Go home, Keegan. It's over. I am not going to the horse center anymore, and the police can take care of things if Nan doesn't return. I want my quiet life, my life with Grandpa. You can get your revenge some other way. No need to hang around me anymore."

He reached for her but she stepped back. The distance between them might as well have been miles.

Tracy, I'm sorry. His heart screamed it but his mouth remained locked in mute anguish.

Tears hovered on the edges of her lashes as she turned and closed the door.

He wanted to pound on it, shout until she let him in so he could explain.

But the truth was, he had used her, partly anyway— before she'd changed from a way to punish his father to a woman he could not imagine life without, a woman he was beginning to love very much indeed.

He couldn't deny it anymore. The irony was bitter. That

he'd realized he loved her at the very moment he'd broken her heart.

"Tracy!" he called.

From inside, he heard the sound of crying.

What have you done, Keegan?

The anger that he'd nursed for so long had broken loose, anger for the woman who'd birthed him, toward the father who'd cast him aside. The losses carved a searing path through his body, twisting him into a man who had used Tracy Wilson and heaped more hurt on his own half brother, adding to their burdens instead of bearing them as God meant him to. He fisted his hand against the door, the rough wood grinding into his knuckles. What had his anger cost him this time?

Not a bloody nose, or problems with a gang, or a broken relationship with his brother.

This time it had cost him his heart.

TWENTY-TWO

Her grandfather mercifully had not pushed her to talk, though she knew he had overheard it all.

I will hang around Tracy forever if it means I can prove Bryce Larraby guilty.

It felt as if she'd been stomach punched.

You're so clueless, Tracy, letting yourself fall in love with a man who was using you the whole time.

After a long, sleepless night, she let herself outside and fed, groomed and spent time with Buttons and Ducky, their playful antics lightening her mood until the hurt crept in again.

She considered her life that had cartwheeled anew when she'd realized she'd fallen in love with a man who was using her. Frost clung to the tall grasses, sparkling on the roofs of the ramshackle cabins she'd planned to turn into a family camp. Would she be able to stay on her property? So close to the Thorn family? Even thinking of Keegan carved an aching path inside that her furry buddies could not dispel.

She finally went in and found her grandfather over-cooking some eggs until they were beyond salvageable.

She tried to eat them anyway, picked at the rubbery whites until he sat beside her at the table and cleared his throat. "You know I've never been so good at the touchy-feely stuff."

She smiled and forced down a lump in her throat. "You don't have to say anything, Grandpa. You were right. I should have listened. He was just using me to get back at his father."

He patted her hand. "Aw, I think maybe you were a little bit right, too. I figure Keegan's a good man, but he's got too many burdens to give you what you deserve."

She nodded, unable to speak.

"And you deserve the best man this world can muster up, Honeybunch."

Now her tears fell because he sounded so much like her father that it almost wrecked her. "I'm glad I have you, Grandpa," she whispered.

"You got an old, cranky codger and I got a sweet, beautiful, bighearted lady, so I'm thinking I got the best out of that deal."

Nestling up next to him, she let the tears flow in earnest, comforted by the feel of his scratchy flannel shirt. When there were no more tears left in her, she cleaned up the dishes while her grandfather took Cyclone outside.

"Gonna scope out which trees we can take down."

"But you're not actually going to tackle that until your ankle's better, right?"

"Don't worry. I ain't gonna chop nothing today, but it don't hurt to start planning. We got a camp to build, don't we?"

She swallowed past the lump of pain in her throat and offered him a smile. "Yes, we do, just the two of us."

He nodded and walked outside.

She sank onto the sofa and checked her phone. There were three texts from Keegan.

Tracy, I'm sorry.
Please forgive me.
I have to talk to you.

There would be no talking. She would likely be able to forgive him someday. The passing of time had a way of blunting resentment, dulling it into something less sharp. It only worked if you didn't keep sharpening the edges of those resentments, cutting and honing over the years until the burdens sliced away at the tender connections inside.

Keegan's anger at Bryce was deadly sharp. She prayed that on some future day, with some other woman, he could finally share his burden. But it wouldn't be with her.

She deleted the texts, closed her eyes and willed herself to focus on the quiet, unobtrusive life she'd meant to live before she'd met the rebellious Keegan Thorn. A buzz from her phone broke her concentration. This time the text was not from Keegan.

I have to meet you.

Who is this? she typed back.

Regina

She started. Regina? She wondered at first how the woman had gotten her cell phone number, but it would not have been much of a task. All of the auction documents listed her number, since her phone was her primary means of contact with clients.

I have to talk to you, to meet you.

What about?

I know the truth about what happened to Nan.

Tracy's mouth went dry.

I'm sorry, but how do I know this is Regina texting me?

She waited for a moment. Then a picture appeared on her phone. It was a selfie of Regina, her face pale and grave. The next photo was a screen shot of the time and date.

Tracy forced a calming breath.

Tell me what you know.

I have to say it in person. I'll meet you at the old barn in Copper Creek tonight at seven.

No. I'm not going to do that.

Please. Bring whoever you want, Keegan, his brothers, I don't care. Just no cops. I'm scared. Leaving tonight right after I talk to you. If you want to know what happened to Nan, it's your only chance.

Tell me now, Tracy tried again. Who killed Nan? Where is her body?

There were no further texts.

Tracy stared at the phone clutched in her ice-cold fingers. The whole thing had trap written all over it, but the lure was so enticing she could not resist thinking it through. If she did not meet Regina, she might never know what had happened to Nan. The rest of her life would be spent with an eye over her shoulder, wondering if the killer was watching, waiting for her memories to return. Unless, of course, the killer was Regina herself.

She walked to the window. Buttons and Ducky cropped grass, tails swishing. Across the pasture she saw Grandpa gazing up at the trees, Cyclone close by, pawing at the tall bushes.

The dream of their campground was all she had left, and what stood between her and realizing it was the truth, buried somewhere deep in her memory.

Tracy knew what she had to do.

She would meet Regina.

But she wouldn't do it alone.

And she'd make certain Keegan wasn't aware of her plan. Whatever they'd had was over.

Time to let go of Keegan Thorn, Tracy.

Keegan worked Outlaw again in the western pasture, and the horse responded brilliantly as ever, but Keegan's heart wasn't in it. He wasn't sure he even wanted to participate in the Friday competition anymore. All he could think about was Tracy and his colossal stupidity.

When he shut the gate behind him and returned to the house, he glanced over at the barn, which was almost ready for Jack's and Owen's weddings. The big doors were slid open. The bows tacked to the benches he and his brothers had crafted were made of something called tulle, his mother had informed him. They fluttered in the cold wind as Ella worked, fastening sprigs of holly handed to her by her sister, Betsy, from the basket on her lap.

A double wedding in a matter of days, he mused. It had been a long time coming. Love hadn't been easy for any of his brothers to find, yet find it they had.

And Keegan had, too. That realization had hit him like a hammer blow between the eyes there on Tracy's doorstep. He'd known he'd admired Tracy, enjoyed her, respected and marveled at her, but he had not realized he loved her, not until the moment he'd buried a knife in her heart and his. He'd been so stupid, so blind; he'd let his past get in the way of his present, just like his brother Jack had said. Pain riveted him to the spot, left him hollow-eyed and staring.

Ella looked up from her work. "Hey, Keeg," she said. "We're going to see the new baby in a few minutes. Want to come?"

"I'll be along in a while," he said, forcing some cheer into his voice. "I hear she's a big one."

"Nine pounds, with an awesome head of hair."

He smiled. "Barrett must be over the moon. Everybody over at the hospital?"

"Just your folks right now."

"Where are Owen and Jack?"

Ella frowned. "Good question. They got a phone call from John, I think. Went on some mysterious mission."

"Where?"

"I don't know, but they took the horses." A flicker of concern crossed her face. "And their rifles. They said something about a mountain lion in the area, but I'm not sure that was the complete truth. Owen sometimes dispenses information on what he feels is a need-to-know basis if he thinks I'll worry."

"Thanks, Ella. See you later."

Hurriedly, he unsaddled Outlaw, rubbed him down and set him loose, before he dialed Jack. No answer, so he tried Owen. Nothing. No reply to texts, either.

Now his blood was ticking faster as he put in a call to John and got his voice mail. He took the truck to town and pulled in at Sunrise Café. No sign of his half brother inside, or any of his cops, so Keegan headed on foot up a block to the police station.

"Chief Larraby isn't here," the receptionist told him.

"Where is he?"

Her forehead creased. "Somewhere else," she answered crisply.

He wasn't going to get anything more from her. Striding toward the exit, he passed an officer sipping coffee from a chipped mug. The cop's radio squawked. Keegan did not hear the message, but he heard the cop's reply.

"Old barn. Got it. I'll watch your six, but stay back on the logging road until your signal. En route."

The officer dumped his coffee with a sigh and hustled out the front door.

Old barn. Logging road.

Keegan knew where it was and his nerves knotted. Furthermore, he knew the easiest way to access the barn if you didn't want to be seen was on horseback, which was what he'd suspected Owen and Jack had done.

John, Owen, Jack. They'd only be working together for one reason.

Tracy.

He sprinted out of the police station and ran back to the café. He'd grabbed the truck's door handle before he noticed the flat tire. And then the other. All four, slashed and useless. Had to be courtesy of Sonny B. Keegan slammed a fist against the door.

He had to get to the barn. His gut told him Tracy was there, and no matter how much backup John had arranged, she was walking into a deadly situation.

A battered truck approached and idled at the curb, engine coughing and sputtering.

Tracy's grandpa jutted his chin at him. "More trouble, I see. Follows you everywhere."

"I've got to get to the old barn in Copper Creek."

Stew lifted an eyebrow. "Tracy arranged some sort of meet-up, didn't she? I gathered as much, but she wouldn't tell me the particulars. Overheard her talking to the cop on the phone."

Keegan grabbed the door. "Mr. Wilson, I need to get to her. She's walking into a trap."

"Cops are there."

"Cops have to follow rules. I don't. I'm a troublemaker, just like you said, and this isn't a 'by the book' scenario."

He glared. "She don't want your help, after what you said. It cut her to the bone."

Keegan let out a long, slow breath. "I don't deserve her, but I can't let her get hurt." He held his breath while the man scrutinized him.

"You know I don't like you."

"Yes, sir."

"And I'd give you the what for if I was a few years younger."

"Yes, sir."

One moment ticked into two. Keegan was ready to explode when Stew Wilson stabbed a finger to the passenger seat. "Get in."

Keegan raced to the door and leaped in.

"Don't think this means I am doing you any favors. Only reason I'm taking you is I want my granddaughter safe."

"I understand, sir," Keegan said, wishing he could take the wheel and floor the accelerator. Instead he shut his mouth, strapped in and prayed it was not too late to save the woman he'd loved and lost.

TWENTY-THREE

Tracy knew Owen and Jack were somewhere in the dense foliage outside the decrepit barn. It comforted her, as well as the fact that John was stationed farther away, watching through binoculars, listening through the earpiece via the device taped to her stomach. Even so, her body felt rubbery, chilled, as she approached the barn.

It was almost sunset and the waning light left the interior in purple shadow. The place smelled of damp hay, rotting wood and an old aroma of livestock. Rusted equipment lay in piles, along with broken crates and mounds of pine needles that had drifted in through holes in the roof.

Tracy licked her dry lips. "Regina? Are you here?"

A scraping noise made her breath catch as Regina stepped out from behind an overturned tractor. Her hands clutched a roll of papers, her mouth screwed up tight. There might have been a trace of tears on her face, but Tracy could not be sure in the poor light.

"Thanks for coming," she said.

"I didn't want to."

"Don't trust me?"

"No," Tracy said.

"I'm not the one you should look out for." She blew

out a breath and Tracy braced herself for whatever she might hear.

"It was Mitch," Regina said, eyes glittering. "He killed Nan. I suspected for a while, but I didn't want to admit it. Now I know."

Tracy's hands were tight fists. "How? How do you know?"

She stared at her feet. "He was supposed to marry me."

"Yes. I'm sorry." She knew what heartbreak felt like, too, but it was not the time to commiserate.

"I began to have suspicions that Mitch was seeing someone else. I talked to Bryce about it. He told me I was being silly, but I think all along he knew Mitch was not being honest. I...I couldn't shake the feeling, so I snooped in Mitch's papers, the ones he keeps in the locked file cabinet in his garage. I found this." She thrust a photo at Tracy. She could barely make out a woman, attractive, older than Regina.

"Look at the earrings."

Tracy peered close. "They're the same ones you have."

"Yeah, they belong to her, Marsha Arnold. His wife." The words fell like stones. "They aren't divorced like he told me. He's been lying, and even had the nerve to give me her earrings." Her tone was pure acid. "I hate him, and I hate myself for being so dumb."

"Oh, Regina," Tracy said. "He's a two-timing jerk, for sure, but that doesn't make him a murderer."

"This does." She thrust a roll of papers at Tracy. "I found these, too. I think he meant to burn them but he hadn't done it yet, or maybe he kept them out of pride, to show how he'd taught Nan a lesson."

Tracy unrolled the papers. "Animal blood tests?"

"Yeah. Mitch has been giving his bulls steroids."

Lost Christmas Memories

Tracy gaped. "To make them meaner?"

"Bigger, meaner, whatever he can do to make them champions. Nan found out. I think she confronted him with the blood tests. He killed her and shoved her body in the crate. Also, I don't know how, but I think he let loose the bulls when you got close to finding her body, or had someone else do it." She shook her head. "I didn't see any of it, but I know he killed Nan."

A wave of nausea swept over Tracy. "No, you didn't see it," she whispered, "but I did."

Images flickered in bursts of light across her mind. The half-concealed figure, the dark eyes, the white teeth. The blurry memory resolved itself into one terrifying image… the face of Mitch Arnold.

Tracy gulped air. "I ran and he followed. He tried to shoot me."

She nodded. "He keeps a gun in his truck at all times."

"He was at the café. He tried to kill me there, too, with chemicals. He knocked over the hay when I was seeing Flight." She shot a look at Regina. "I thought it was you."

Regina's lip trembled. "I'm a lot of things, but I'm not a killer. As soon as Mitch knows I came to you, he'll be after me, too. I have to go."

"No," Tracy said, grabbing her wrist. "The police will need your testimony."

"I'm done. I'm leaving."

"Please…" Tracy said.

Something clanked above their heads. She had a split second to see Mitch rising from the hayloft. With a sickening lurch, she realized he'd gotten there ahead of them, waiting to see what kind of evidence Regina had against him. Before she could react, he lobbed a metallic canister, which tumbled down, trailing a thick plume of smoke.

* * *

Keegan was out and running up the trail before the truck had come to a complete stop. Smoke drifted against the darkening sky. A fire? John stepped from behind his car, half concealed in the bushes. Keegan made to go around him when John's partner grabbed Keegan and pinned his arms behind his back. Keegan fought hard, but the cop held fast.

"She's in trouble!" he shouted. "Let me help."

"We have cops moving in. Likely a smoke bomb. Looks like Mitch got here first."

"Tracy…"

"You're staying here. I'll report when I can."

"Let me go with you."

"Not a chance."

And why should John give Keegan what he wanted when Keegan had maligned him at every turn? He hadn't thought John credited anything Tracy said, but now he realized he'd been wrong, dead wrong, about many things.

He heaved out a breath and marshaled his thoughts, readying himself to say what he thought would never pass from his own lips. "Please, John. You're right—I wanted so bad to punish Bryce and maybe you, too, that I was a jerk. I used Tracy and I didn't see the truth about Mitch because I was so busy looking elsewhere." His breath caught. "And I blamed you for things that I shouldn't have." Panic pricked his insides. "Tracy can't pay for my idiocy. Please, John, I know I don't deserve your consideration, but I'm asking anyway. Please let me help you find her."

John looked at Keegan, expression unreadable.

"I didn't see it, either, about Mitch," John said. He nodded to the other cop to let Keegan go.

For the first time in his life, Keegan would partner with his half brother instead of battle him.

"Thank you," he said. He'd never meant the words as much as he did then.

John shrugged and grabbed a rifle. He sent his officer to call for more units before he and Keegan raced toward the smoking barn.

Tracy crouched low and pulled Regina down next to her. Mitch's diversion could work to their advantage. "Keep under the smoke. We'll get out the front, and the cops or the Thorn brothers will help us."

Regina gripped her hand and together they crept toward the door. Tracy could not see Mitch, but she figured they had a few minutes while he climbed down from the hayloft.

The door was only a few feet away when Regina fell over a rusted rake. She went down with a shriek that gave away their location. Tracy pulled her up and shoved her toward the big sliding door. Half tripping, they moved closer until Tracy could feel the cool night air. Only a little farther...

"This is the police." The announcement broke the silence like a gunshot. "Mitch Arnold, come out of the barn slowly, with your hands up."

Regina looked at Tracy. "Will they shoot us by mistake?"

Tracy texted John. "I just told him we're coming out."

Suddenly, Mitch loomed up behind them and gave Regina a mighty shove, which sent her reeling out into the night. Tracy tried to scramble after her, but Mitch grabbed her by the arms and hauled her back into the barn.

"We're going out another way," he said. "You and I have unfinished business."

She tried to drag her feet, tried to scream, but he was so much stronger that her boots scuffled ineffectually across the wood floor. Smoke swirled all around her, and she could not see where Mitch meant to take her until he'd pulled her out a gaping hole in the wall of the barn.

Again she tried to twist free, to scratch at him, to claw with her fingers, but he yanked her firmly away. The Thorn brothers had likely not seen the hole, and John would be distracted by Regina's appearance out the front.

"Let go of me," she said, fighting for all she was worth. He tried to clamp a hand over her mouth but she bit down hard. Grumbling an oath, he pinned her to his side and fished for something in his pocket.

It was her moment, maybe her only moment, and she jerked hard, loosening his grip. Elation surged through her until he hooked a boot around her ankle and brought her to the ground. A needle stabbed into her neck. Her cry was muffled by the forest debris as the injected drug began to dim her senses.

"Horse tranquilizer," he said into her ear. "See how you like that, honey." With rough fingers, he felt around her waist and yanked free the transmitter that had been taped there. Then he snatched the papers from her back pocket: Nan Ridley's proof, the facts and figures that had signed Nan's death warrant. As Tracy's vision went black, she wondered if the papers would prove to be her death warrant, too.

Keegan reached Regina first, in spite of John calling him off. "Where's Tracy?"

"He's got her." Regina panted. "Mitch."

Keegan ran into the barn, searching through the smoke, but there was no sign of Tracy. Jack and Owen charged in with John.

Jack shook his head. "They didn't come out the back. We had that covered."

Keegan prowled the whole space again, heart whamming against his ribs until the smoke dissipated enough for him to make out the hole. "He took her that way."

Tracy's grandfather hobbled into the barn. "Where is she?"

Keegan desperately did not want to tell him, but he would not lie to the man Tracy held dearest in the world.

"Mitch has her."

"Mitch Arnold? He's the one who killed the veterinarian?"

"It looks that way," John said. He spoke to his partner. "Get Mr. Wilson and Miss Parker back to the car and keep them there."

"What are you going to do?" the old man asked. John might have assumed the question was meant for him, but Grandpa Stew's eyes were fastened on Keegan. He understood the man's unspoken thoughts as he grabbed Keegan's wrist with shaking fingers, squeezing hard.

You are responsible. If she dies, it's on your head.

It would be on his head, and in his heart forever, if anything happened to Tracy Wilson.

Without a word, he leaped through the hole and charged out into the woods to find her.

TWENTY-FOUR

Tracy's arms and legs were limp and useless. She was barely clinging to consciousness enough to know that Mitch had her over his shoulder and they were deep in the trees, far from the barn. Branches swung dizzyingly around her, grabbing at her hair, stabbing at her back.

Whatever drug he'd injected her with did nothing to dull her terror. He'd killed Nan and now he would murder her, also. She tried to kick, to wriggle, but it was as if she were buried deep underground, immobilized. The forest floor became muddy, sticking to Mitch's boots as he carried her.

Finally the trees thinned and she realized with a sickening lurch that they had come to the edge of a rocky ridge that looked down into a wide expanse of lake. The water was probably no more than fifteen feet across and she didn't know how deep, but it didn't really matter anyway. There was enough to drown her, and that was exactly what Mitch intended to do.

He slid her to the ground and knelt next to her.

"You stuck your nose into my business, just like Nan. Two busybody women, all right. And Regina, too, but I think she's gonna have the good sense to get out of town the minute she can after your body is found. Almost worked, that plan."

"They…they know…" was all she could get out.

"Got me a little nest egg put away, Miss Wilson. I don't want to leave this place, it was a real good gig here, but I'll get started somewhere else." He laughed. "Different name, different town, different women, same racket. Still, though, a man's gotta settle his debt, and you did me wrong by butting in and ruining things for me, so in you go, Miss Wilson. Drown quickly or slowly. I don't really care."

He grabbed her under the shoulders and heaved her to the edge of the water. She clutched at the branches, rocks, anything, but she could not stop the terrible progress.

Slowly, inexorably, he moved her toward the edge.

"Get a good look," he breathed in her ear. "Drowning must be a real bad way to go. Helpless while the water fills your lungs, but your brain works right up to the end, I hear. Your brain knows you're dying but your body can't do a thing about it."

Frantic now, she kicked out, managed to get one of her legs to move, but not enough.

She thought of her grandfather, the dream they'd had that would never be realized. An image of Keegan rose in her mind. Another dream, one she had not even known she'd wanted, ended before it began. And her mother and sister—why hadn't the Lord helped her reconcile with them in time? Tears threatened but she blinked them back. She would not give Mitch her tears. If that was the only thing she could do to resist, then she'd bottle up those tears tight where he could not see.

Once more, she dug her feet into the ground and prayed.

Keegan had gone hunting with his adopted granddad countless times. He'd become a skilled tracker, but it was dark and his nerves were firing a mile a minute.

Jack and Owen had each ridden off on different search

routes, one toward the logging road and the other look-ing for Mitch's vehicle, which must be hidden somewhere close. Grandpa Stew and the deputy had gone with Regina back to the safety of the squad car, though Stew had pro-tested angrily.

John had brought two flashlights and handed one to Keegan.

"There," Keegan said, stabbing a finger at the broken branches. "He took her this way."

They plunged into the thick branches, Keegan beaming the flashlight at the ground and bushes.

"Left," he directed, moving them onto a faint scratch of a trail.

"I called in backup," John murmured. "They're en route."

They'd be too late. Tracy's only chance at life would be gone in the next few minutes if they didn't find her.

They came to a spot where the trail branched into two.

"Which way?" John asked.

Keegan scanned frantically. Wrong choice and she died. Sweat stung his eyes. "I can't tell." He got on his knees, examining the ground as John played his flashlight over the earth. No broken twigs, no bruised branches, no marks at all. "I don't know."

"We'll split up," John said.

Keegan was getting to his feet when he saw it, the par-tial print of a boot heel in the damp earth.

"This way." His throat seized up as realization hit him. "He's taking her to the lake."

They ran now, heedless of the noise they made until they pulled up, panting, behind a thick hedge. Peering from the cover of the tangled branches, Keegan saw Mitch pushing something toward the edge. His gut clenched. Tracy. He jerked forward but John stopped him.

"Give me thirty seconds to get a bead on him."

"No, I…" With everything in him, he wanted to go right at Mitch and run him down like a wild stallion, but something inside, something new, told him to listen to his brother.

"Thirty seconds," John repeated.

Keegan nodded and John whirled away into the foliage. Thirty…twenty…fifteen…

Keegan could hardly keep his body in place. Tracy… was she alive? Had he taken too long to find her?

Ten…five…

When he hit one, he exploded from the bushes with a roar, just as Mitch pushed Tracy into the water. Mitch jerked to a standing position and took off. Keegan desperately wanted to go after him, but he careened down the slope and plunged into the frigid water, fingers scrambling to find Tracy.

The wind teased movement into the lake and so much mud had stirred from the bottom that he could not see her. Tossing off his hat, he went under, hands outstretched as the seconds ticked by. The cold water sapped the breath from him. No Tracy.

Breaking the surface, he looked again for a sign of where she'd gone in, but the darkness worked against him.

"Tracy!" he shouted.

He heard it, the tiniest splash, from her foot or maybe her hand, but it was enough for him to make a grab, his fingers finding the sleeve of her jacket. Elated, he pulled her out of the water. She was coughing, sputtering, and he thanked God for the weak noises as he cradled her to his chest.

She was crying and he held her tight.

"You're all right, Pockets," he said, hardly able to breathe himself. "You're gonna be all right."

* * *

Keegan had carried Tracy back to the clearing, where they'd met up with a waiting ambulance. The medics had whisked her away immediately, and he'd yearned to follow, but John had not yet returned, nor had Jack. Grandpa Stew departed for the hospital after the medics had given them some assurance that Tracy's vitals were good.

Owen threw a blanket around Keegan's shoulders and gripped his arm.

"Thanks," Keegan said. "I—"

Owen squeezed, cutting off words he must have known would be an apology. "Save it. Soon as John's back, we'll take you to the hospital to be with her."

The other apology he needed to make would not go as well. He'd been wrong about his father. Dead wrong. Bryce Larraby was innocent.

A second ambulance arrived and Keegan was further relieved when John appeared in the clearing, unharmed, followed by Jack, with his rifle over his shoulder.

"I shot Mitch," John said flatly. "He gave me no choice. Jack cut him off from getting to his vehicle, and he refused to surrender. My men are with him. He's alive, so far."

Keegan nodded. "You were right, about your plan to save Tracy."

John raised an eyebrow. "That's twice you've told me I'm right recently. I'm beginning to suspect a head injury."

Keegan chuckled. John's phone rang and he answered, listening intently before he clicked off. "They found Nan Ridley's body in the woods about a mile from the center. She was concealed under a pile of logs. Mitch must have transported her by car, which threw off the dogs. The coroner won't have an official time of death for a while, but he guesses she's been dead since last Wednesday."

Keegan blew out a breath. "The day Tracy saw Mitch murder her at the center."

"Yeah," John said. "I should have believed her."

A car slammed to a halt and Bryce got out. He hastened over. "What happened? I heard sirens. Fire department said the barn was smoking but not burning. What is going on?"

John explained as Bryce's eyes widened.

"So Mitch murdered Nan and hid her body?"

"Yes." John blew out a breath. "I shot him as he tried to escape."

"Is he…dead?"

"Not yet, but he's in bad shape. Lost a lot of blood."

Bryce scrubbed a hand over his face. "Well," he said after a moment, "at least it's over." He glared at Keegan. "And all this time you've been trying to insinuate I was a murderer."

Keegan sucked in the biggest breath of his life. "I was wrong."

"You were more than just wrong," he snapped, cheeks flushing. "You've slandered my name and my business. It was all out of spite because I wouldn't claim you as my own."

Keegan silently took the ire he knew he had coming.

John shifted uncomfortably.

"That was the best decision of my life," Bryce said.

Keegan swallowed. Hard.

"The accusations, the rumors you've spread." Bryce shook his head, triumph in his eyes. "You might have had the whole world believing I killed Nan and hid her body under a woodpile."

Keegan frowned as Bryce went on.

"The horse show is going to be a success in spite of you. At least I can hang on to that. I put everything I had into the center. I'm glad to know it was worth the gamble. You didn't win, Keegan. How does it feel?"

John, too, was staring at Bryce now.

"What?" Bryce said. "What's the matter with you two? Why are you staring?"

"Dad…" John began. "I just now got the call about Nan's body. No one could know that it was found underneath a woodpile except…"

"For the person who put it there," Keegan finished.

Bryce stopped, mouth open, all the vitality draining from his expression. "I…I didn't…"

"The truth, Dad," John said. "Because I'm going to have my cops all over your house, your center, your car inside an hour."

Bryce's round-eyed gaze drifted back and forth between Keegan and John. "I…I was at the horse center to meet Tracy on that Wednesday night. I heard a scuffle and saw Mitch take off after her. In the office I found…" He swallowed. "I found Nan's body. It would have ruined everything, you see. Ruined the show, a thing like that."

"What did you do?" John said, voice low and throbbing with emotion.

"I…" Bryce looked helplessly from Keegan to John. "It would have ruined everything," he repeated.

Keegan felt like he'd been punched in the gut. "So you hid Nan's body in the crate and told Mitch to keep his mouth shut. You arranged to clean up the scene, even the broken ornament."

"I didn't kill her. I'm not a murderer."

"No," John said, hurt hardening the lines around his mouth. "But you obstructed justice and protected a killer. Did you know about Mitch's plans to kill Tracy? Maybe even helped him?"

Bryce's voice came out as a whisper. "I knew…but I

didn't help. That was all him." He swallowed again. "I couldn't let her ruin everything."

Keegan's brain could not believe what his ears were hearing. "You helped Mitch get away with killing Nan and you would have let him do the same to Tracy?"

Bryce went still, looking from Keegan to John. "I think I won't say anything else until I talk to a lawyer."

John took a pair of cuffs from his belt. "You can call one from jail."

Keegan watched John read Bryce his rights and load him into the back seat of the car.

Before his half brother slid into the driver's seat, Keegan gripped John's forearm.

"I'm sorry. I thought this is what I wanted…but it isn't. I'm sorry."

John bowed his head and let out a long breath. When he looked up again, there was no longer bitterness between them, only a shared sadness. "Me, too."

Maybe, thought Keegan as John drove away, Bryce had helped build a fragile bridge between him and his brother in spite of himself. Keegan resolved to do his part to keep it standing.

Bone-tired and flesh-weary, he trudged toward his brothers who stood ready to get him to the hospital.

Tracy hoped she would never again set foot in a hospital. Her Saturday—Christmas Eve—homecoming had been filled with warm hugs from her grandfather and licks from Cyclone, who seemed to have taken up permanent residence at the property. There were no lingering effects from the horse sedative Mitch had administered except fatigue and a nagging headache.

Keegan had been there at the hospital through it all, smuggling in cookies for her and stroking her hair, dry-ing her tears, until she'd finally been discharged. Why? Guilt, probably. She still wasn't sure where things stood with Keegan, but she did not have the energy to try to muddle through it. She was alive and Nan could be laid to rest, and that was enough to hold on to.

She was surprised to see Buttons and Ducky both sporting Christmas bandannas, and some fresh pine decorating the fence. Her grandfather beamed. "Cute little rascals, aren't they?"

She laughed and kissed him, settling into her cozy cabin with only a small pang as she eyed the Christmas tree Keegan had provided.

After a long nap and a hot shower, Tracy's phone buzzed with a text message.

Tracy stared at the phone, her breathing suspended.

"What is it, Honeybunch?"

"It's from Mom. She says… I mean, I asked if I could bring over the bead bracelets I'd made for her and Lily, and she said…"

Her throat suddenly closed up, so Grandpa took the phone from her hand and read the screen. "'We are home. A visit would be nice.'"

Eight words and her heart felt as light as the shimmering winter sunshine. It was almost enough to send her into gales of laughter. All the pieces of her life had fallen into place, except when she thought of a certain blue-eyed cowboy.

I will hang around Tracy forever if it means I can prove Bryce Larraby guilty. And now Bryce was guilty and Keegan had no reason to stay close, other than an attack of conscience. Maybe he'd assuaged that with his hospital ministrations. Again, her throat clogged with unshed tears.

The knock startled her. At first terror prevented her

from moving until she told herself firmly that Mitch and Bryce were under arrest. She was safe; she was free.

She opened the door to find Keegan holding a massive bundle of sunflowers in one hand and a bunch of carrots in the other. He wore black jeans, a tucked-in button-up shirt and a leather jacket.

"Hey," he said, peering around the flowers.

She realized her mouth was open. "Well, um, hi. I thought you'd be busy with the wedding."

"I am. Mama sent me to town to get a haircut, which I didn't need, but in the spirit of Christmas I got it anyway. Plus she said since I ate all the cream puffs for the dessert buffet, it was my responsibility to go get more if I knew what was good for me, so I'm on my way back from town."

He looked down at the ground. "Tracy, what I said before, about staying with you so I could prove my father guilty…" He blew out a breath. "I'm sorry. I wish I could say it wasn't true, but I think I was using you."

"You don't have to…" His eyes rose to hers, pained and tender.

"But that's only part of it, the part I've been praying about. The other part, I mean, I…well." He shook his head as if to clear it and then thrust the sunflowers at her. "Here. I wanted to get roses, but Mama has commandeered every single rose in town for the reception, so here are some sunflowers and…" The last bit came out in a rush. "Would you please be my date for the wedding?"

She blinked. "Oh, I don't think…"

His expression was dead serious. "I know I messed up, and by all rights you should slam the door in my face, but I am asking anyway. Please come with me. Let me show you what kind of man I can be. Please. Just one date."

She gazed at the sunflowers. "Keegan, it's not a good idea."

He sighed. "If you don't go, I will be the only lonely soul there available to hold the baby, and I'm scared of infants. You gotta save me."

She could not hold back a laugh at that. "Okay. One date. When should I be ready?"

A dazzling smile broke over him. "Excellent. I'll pick you up at three o'clock. Bring a jacket, 'cause the barn is chilly. Grandpa is invited, too," he said, tossing the words over his shoulder as he jogged down the driveway.

"Keegan?" she called.

"Yeah?"

"Did you bring those carrots for some reason or just in case you needed a snack?"

He eyed the cluster in his hand. "Oh, yeah. Forgot all about it. Christmas gift for Buttons and Ducky." He handed her the carrots and kissed her cheek before she knew it was coming. His lips sent shivers up her spine.

One date, she told herself. Just one date.

Keegan could not believe the barn could be so transformed. He ushered folks to their seats, amid the bows and roses and grinning brothers.

Shelby sat in the front row, baby bundled in her lap, next to Evie and Tom, and Barrett could not take his eyes off his wife or their daughter. Jack and Owen were similarly transfixed by their brides, Shannon and Ella, one tall and dark-haired, the other small with fiery red curls, and both lovely in white gowns, holding bouquets, complemented by the pomanders the bridesmaids held. But Keegan was enchanted by a different woman in the room.

Tracy wore a simple pink dress that hugged her slender waist and brought out blooms on her cheeks. Her blond hair was piled into some sort of soft arrangement that highlighted the hazel of her eyes, the satin of her skin. He showed her to her seat, Grandpa Stew settling next to her in a plaid shirt and bolo tie.

"Hey," Grandpa Stew said, "I don't think you'll be having any more trouble from that Sonny B fella."

Keegan stared at him. "How's that?"

"What did you do?" Tracy demanded.

"Aw, he came up on the property on his motorcycle again while you two was getting all gussied up for the wedding. Turns out that was him on the property before, you know, not Mitch. I shot out both his tires and told him I was gonna tell everyone in town he got bested by an old man with a bum leg. Gonna shame him six ways to Sunday to anyone who would listen. He couldn't run down the road fast enough. Heard he left town."

Keegan laughed so loud he earned a startled look from his mother. "Thank you, sir."

"Don't let it go to your head. I still don't like you."

"Yes, sir, I know."

But there was a smile on her grandpa's wrinkled face, the same smile he'd sported when Keegan had taken him aside just before the ceremony started.

The pastor started the proceedings and the wedding began. From the reciting of the vows to the exchanging of the rings, everything went exactly as the Thorn women had planned.

Before Keegan knew it, the ceremony was over and the reception had begun. He broke from the group and beelined straight for Tracy, helping her on with her sweater. "Let's go outside," he whispered to her. "I think I see Shelby coming at me with the baby."

She giggled. "I like babies."

"They're scary and they leak," he said, waving at someone across the assembled tables clustered next to the heat lamps.

John lifted a mug of cider to return the greeting.

"I'm surprised to see him here," she said.

"Really, you're surprised I'm not sniping at him."

She smiled. "Well, yes, actually."

Keegan ran a hand through his hair. "I guess with all that's happened, I learned a few things," he said. "Let go of a few of my own burdens long enough to take note of other people's."

She went quiet, studying him in a way that made his nerves race. "I am so glad."

"I'm not a new man or anything," he said. "I'm the same thrill-seeking hothead, but..." He looked at his mother, who gazed, teary-eyed, at her sons and their new wives and the tiny squirming infant. "I'm a better version of myself... thanks to you."

"No," Tracy said, "I just got you into trouble."

"You got me out of it, made me see myself for what I was, how I treated people, how I treated you."

She looked away. "I'm glad I met you."

He touched her chin and brought her eyes back to look at him. "You are what I need in my life and I..." He cleared his throat. "I know I can be what you need. I love you, Tracy."

Now her eyes went wide. "Keegan, I know you want to mean that, but I think you're mistaken about your feelings. We haven't known each other that long."

"Nope. I'm mistaken about a lot of things, and I imagine I'll make huge, colossal, mind-bending mistakes in the future, but on this I'm not, Pockets. You are the person I've been looking for my whole life—you are the woman I want to be my partner now and forever."

The sparkle of Christmas lights danced across her face as the band struck up a medley of carols.

"You're my gift, Tracy. I want to be yours, too."

Her lips pressed together and he tapped her sweater. "What you got in there, Pockets?"

Openmouthed with surprise, she reached into her pocket and pulled out a black-velvet box. He took it from her and opened it, removing the delicate band inset with a small diamond.

"Best I could afford, much smaller than you deserve. I know you have your dream, you and your grandpa, and I want to help you make that campground the best in the county. I already asked your grandpa for permission to propose, by the way. He said he still doesn't like me, but he gave his consent." He kissed her knuckle. "We can make some dreams of our own, too, if you'll have me." He slid the ring on her finger, and through his haze of near panic, he realized she had let him.

"But it's so soon…"

"We can be engaged as long as you like. Whatever you need." He sank to one knee. "Will you marry me, Tracy?" he whispered.

She cupped his cheeks in her warm hands and bent her head to touch his. Her caress was gentle as a spring breeze and filled with a forever promise. "Yes," she murmured, nose to nose with him. "Yes, I will. I love you, Keegan."

"I love you, too, Pockets." Keegan rose to embrace her, kissing her as many times as she'd let him before she pushed at his chest.

"Everyone is staring," she whispered.

He turned and found all four of his brothers grinning at him, as well as his mom and dad and the guests.

"Looks like we've got another wedding to plan," Evie said, wiping away tears.

"Better start rustling up food now," Jack added. "The Iron Cowboy here can eat more than a hundred guests can."

Keegan laughed and grabbed a glass of cider for him and Tracy. He held his glass up high.

"Thank You, God, for Your gift to us," he said, and everyone raised their glasses. "And thank You for this family," he added, gazing at Tracy, his Christmas gift for now and forever.

* * * * *

If you enjoyed Lost Christmas Memories, *look for the other books in the Gold Country Cowboys series:*

Cowboy Christmas Guardian
Treacherous Trails
Cowboy Bodyguard

Dear Reader,

I just love a good cowboy story, don't you? It has been such fun to write the Thorn brothers' stories, from oldest, Barrett, to youngest brother, Keegan. Throughout the series, Keegan has struggled to feel a sense of belonging, to find a place where he feels loved and valued. We all search for that kind of place, don't we? Isn't it nice to know that God has a room waiting for us where we will be fully loved and completely accepted? I can't imagine a happier ending than that!

It has been my pleasure to gallop with you through Gold Country in this four-book series. I hope you will come along with me on the next adventure, too! As always, I love to hear from my readers. You can contact me via my website at www.danamentink.com and there's a place to sign up for my quarterly newsletter. There is also a post office box listed below. Thanks again, dear readers, and God bless you!

Dana Mentink

P.O. Box 3168
San Ramon, CA 94583

Get 4 FREE REWARDS!

We'll send you 2 FREE Books plus 2 FREE Mystery Gifts.

Love Inspired® Suspense books feature Christian characters facing challenges to their faith... and lives.

FREE Value Over $20

Toby Potter watched the flames shoot toward the sky as he raced toward the building. "Robin!"

Sirens screamed closer. Toby had been on his way home when he'd spotted Robin's car in the parking lot of the lab. Ever since Robin had discovered his deception—orders to get close to her and figure out what was going on in the lab—she'd kept him at arm's length, her narrow-eyed stare hot enough to singe his eyebrows if he dare try to get too close.

Tonight, he'd planned to apologize profusely—again—and ask if there was anything he could do to earn her trust back. Only to pull into the parking lot, be greeted by the loud boom and watch flames shoot out of the window near the front door.

Heart pounding, Toby scanned the front door and rushed forward only to be forced back by the intense heat. Smoke billowed toward the dark night sky while the fire grew hotter and bigger. Mini explosions followed. Chemicals.

"Robin!"

Toby jumped into his truck and drove around to the back only to find it not much better, although it did seem to be more smoke than flames. Robin was in that building, and he was afraid he'd failed to protect her. Big-time.

Toby parked near the tree line in case more explosions were coming.

At the back door, he grasped the handle and pulled. Locked. Of course. Using both fists, he pounded on the glass-and-metal door. "Robin!"

Another explosion from inside rocked Toby back, but he was able to keep his feet under him. He figured the blast was on the other end of the building—where he knew Robin's station was. If she was anywhere near that station, there was no way she was still alive. "No, please no," he whispered. No one was around to hear him, but maybe God was listening.

Don't miss
Holiday Amnesia by Lynette Eason,
available December 2018 wherever
Love Inspired® Suspense books and ebooks are sold.

www.LoveInspired.com